Seek and Ye Sl

Seek and Ye Shall Find Me

Annette McGarill

Albion Publications
Email: albionpublications@gmail.com

ISBN 978-1-5272-7964-3

Cover Design: Straightline Creative
Email: mark.mclaren@straightline.me
Printed by: The Evolve Group
Email: info@theevolvegroup.co.uk

For all my families – past, present and to come.

Acknowledgements

Thanks to everyone who encouraged me to write this and assisted me along the way: to my partner, John, for his advice, help with research, and technical assistance; to my daughters, Susan and Siobhan, for always believing in me; to my good friends Alex, Ann, Avril, Mary and Vicky for feedback and support; to Dr Linda Jackson for editing my work and for helpful practical advice. I also want to thank the Mitchell Library staff for assistance with family history research; Quarriers for providing well-preserved, detailed nineteenth-century records and the Ontario East British Home Child Family for help with tracking child migrants and their families in Canada.

1

Glasgow, March 1878

Jane grasped her brother's hand as they trudged along the wet, filthy ground in the dark. Fog swirled around them, brushing their clothes and faces like ghostly fingers. 'We're almost there; not long now', said John. Her feet ached as she struggled to keep on what was left of her shoes. John had mended them as best he could, but the winter weather had been too much for the flimsy material - scraps he had gathered at his work. If only her father were still alive, he could have made her a new pair. She could see him in her mind, crouching over his shoemaker's last while he skilfully cut and stitched the leather he worked with: how she had loved to watch him as shoes seemed to appear at his fingertips. But he was gone - dead in the cold earth at Dalbeth. She tried to imagine his voice but could only hear the rasping cough and laboured breaths of his last few weeks, before his breath stopped. She hoped he was in Heaven, strong again and happy: maybe he'd met her mother there. She hoped so, but dearly wished she could have them both back: wanted the happiness they had all shared. Her mother's face was hard to imagine now but she could remember the warmth of her.

'Coorie in, ma wee pet', she would say when Jane crept into the big bed in the recess: she went there to escape the cold and discomfort of the floor in front of the fireplace once the embers had burnt out. For as long as she could remember, she had shared threadbare mats with her brothers. When James went to sea and John went to live with Auld Slowey, the shoemaker, to learn his trade, the mats seemed like an empty boat on a cold and lonely sea. When her mother had become ill and she couldn't go to her, how alone she had felt. Now Ma too was dead and the house only a distant memory, fading fast.

'You know I'd keep you with me if I could, don't you, Jane? Auld Slowey is good enough to me and I'm glad to be learning to be a shoemaker like Da, but there is hardly room for me there. I sleep in the lobby with other boys and it's all very cramped.'

'I know, John. Maybe when you're able to leave and work for yourself you can come for me.' Jane's lip trembled. 'What is this place I'm going to?'

'It's the Orphans' Home and they'll look after you, I promise. You'll still be in Calton, so we'll not be far away. And it won't be forever. Ellen will be home soon and you might be able to go back to her.' John feared this was unlikely but he wanted to comfort his young sister. Ellen, the eldest in the family, was in Duke Street Prison for stealing food to feed her own children and Jane. Caught several times before, she would not be allowed out this time till some months had passed. Her husband was barely able to look after their own children and Jane was now an impossible burden to add to his troubles. Her being there had seemed like a solution when first their father, then their mother had died and Jane had been put in the Poorhouse. Ellen had taken her from that miserable place, not fit for animals, and tried to care for her but now Jane would have to go into the Home to have any chance of surviving. He didn't want her to end up living on the streets like the other children he saw, ragged and hungry and cold in the harsh Glasgow weather. He squeezed her hand, promising himself he would get her back when he could.

Up ahead loomed a tall, dark building with lots of windows: dim lights flickered behind them, hazy through the rain and fog.

'We're here', said John. Jane stopped, terror-stricken now that the Home was in sight.

'Do I have to go?' John stooped down and cuddled her.

'Ye'll be safe here, Jane. Be a brave lassie and mind how good Ma and Da wanted you to be. Think of them and it will be easier.' Jane thought of them and felt her heart would break.

Holding onto her, John approached a large wooden door and raised the knocker on it. As it banged down, the noise seemed to echo the beating of Jane's heart. After a few moments, the door was opened by a woman in a long grey dress and apron. She peered at them through the rain.

'What's your business here?'

'My sister has nowhere to live. Our parents are dead and I hear tell that you look after orphans.' Jane huddled against him, wishing she could disappear.

'Can you take her in?'

'Come away in. I cannae tell you now - 'tis not my place - but wait here till I speak to the Maister.' They stepped inside a hallway lit by gas lamps which cast an eerie glow: shadows moved around the walls and floor.

The woman went through a door off the hallway and they could hear voices. Jane wanted to run, but where would she go? Some other family lived in their house now. Ellen's house was better than the street, but she had not been happy there: she loved Ellen but her husband, Henry, was frightening and treated her harshly. Ellen said he was sick and couldn't work. Jane had helped with the children, but at seven she was not much older than they were and found it hard. Now Ellen was in that awful place, Duke Street Prison, where she would have to do hard work in the prison yard as her punishment. The real punishment would be not seeing her children or knowing how they were. If she could do something to help her Jane would, but Henry didn't want her there, and, if truth be told, she had been glad when John at last came for her and she could leave, wishing he could take her to live with him, but knowing that couldn't happen.

John and Jane looked nervously around the room. There was a large iron fireplace and near it a desk and chair; the fire was out and the room was chilly, but warmer than the streets. The door then opened, and the woman who had let them in held it ajar for a tall man in dark clothing. He glanced at Jane then spoke to John, looking at him with piercing eyes.

'I am Mr Galbraith of the Orphan Homes of Glasgow. Who is this child? What is she to you?' John sounded a little scared when he answered,

'Sir, she's my sister, Jane. I'm John Anderson and our parents are both dead. I cannot look after her myself but I want her to be cared for. She has been in the Poorhouse before and came out quite ill. My wee brother died in there and I don't think she will survive if she goes back.'

'Why can't you look after her yourself?'

'I'm an apprentice shoemaker and bide with my master. He will not have her there.'

'No other brothers or sisters?'

'Sir, my brother James is at sea.' He hesitated, but under the man's watchful gaze went on, 'We have a sister but she has children of her own and her man is sick. She did keep Jane for a while but cannot keep her now.'

'Why not?'

'Sir, she was trying to get food for the family but had no money. She was...taken away.'

'Taken away to where?' John blushed and stammered.

'To Duke Street Prison, Sir.'

'I see. Well in time this little one might have followed in her ways, so I will try to save her from that. As her parents are dead, we can keep her for now. We have a bed which has just become available and she will be fed, but the child will need to work in the Home and do as she is bidden.'

'She is a good girl, Sir, and will do what is asked of her.' Jane clung to John's hand, trying to hold back her tears. The man at last spoke to her.

'Will you be good, Jane? Do you know of God who watches over all of us and knows what is in our hearts?'

'Yes.' She wondered if God knew she wanted to stay with John, and looked down at the floor lest Mr Galbraith should read the truth in her eyes.

'Well, we will see. You must go now and wash before bed. John, you must give me all of the particulars about Jane. Mr Quarrier who owns the Home needs to have them.' Mr Galbraith sat at a desk and took up paper and a pen. He pulled a cord on the wall beside the fireplace and, a moment later, an older woman appeared and curtsied before him.

'Take Jane to be washed and clothed. I trust she can have supper before bed.'

'Yes, Sir.'

'Well, say goodbye to your brother, child.' Jane looked desperately at John and could not let him go.

'Jane, it's for the best. I'll come back for you when I can.'
The woman stepped forward and pulled Jane towards her, but spoke kindly. 'Come, Jane, you will feel better once you are settled.' She took Jane's hand from John's and led her to the door. The tears came then though Jane tried to be brave. Her lip trembled as she said,

'Come soon, John, and tell Ellen where I am.'

'I will.' Her last sight of John was of him standing with his hand to his head, holding back his own tears. The door closed between them and Jane turned to face the unknown.

The woman held Jane's hand tightly as if afraid she would run back to her brother. 'My name is Miss Mathieson; I am the housekeeper here. We are going to get you cleaned, and then you can have something to eat.' They walked along a cold corridor to a door marked, 'Bathroom'. Jane sounded out the unfamiliar word in her head. Inside stood a row of sinks against one wall and two large tin baths in the middle of the floor; at the back of the room was a huge wooden cupboard; large jugs were laid out on a wooden bench against another wall. Miss Mathieson took a jug, saying, 'I'll fetch some hot water from the kitchen. Stay here.' Jane stood as if paralysed.

When Miss Mathieson returned, she poured water from the jug into a bath and the steam from it seemed to float around the room. She added some cold water from a spigot above a sink. 'That should do nicely. Take off your clothes and get in.' Jane was embarrassed at removing her clothes in front of a stranger, but Miss Mathieson was busy looking in the cupboard. As Jane climbed into the bath, she turned and gave her a block of strong-smelling red soap. 'Use this to wash all over - I'll do your hair.' Jane thought of her mother, and how washing had taken place at the jawbox in the scullery, the whole family sharing what precious water they had: it was often cold if they had no coal or wood to light the stove. Despite Jane's fear and embarrassment, she was enjoying the feeling of this warm water on her body. She washed and the water clouded and hid her lower half, so she felt more at ease. Miss Mathieson used the soap for her hair, then poured clean water over it before adding vinegar from a large bottle to the water and rinsing it for a final time. She told Jane to get out and handed her a small sheet of coarse cotton to dry herself: the rough material seemed to make her blood run faster. Miss Mathieson picked up Jane's clothes and flung them in a corner, saying,

'These will need to be destroyed: they are filthy, but you may keep your shoes till we find proper boots for you. What age are you?'

'Seven, Miss.' From the cupboard the housekeeper took underclothes, drawers and a petticoat, stockings and two brown shifts which she held against Jane to try for size.

'You're small for seven, but these will do.' Jane quickly put on the clothes, feeling very strange. Even her shoes felt different, squeezed over the thick stockings instead of her bare feet. She then had to stand before

7

Miss Mathieson while her hair was combed through and checked 'for head lice or nits'. Miss Mathieson seemed satisfied that there were neither, though Jane's head felt raw where the hard comb had scraped across her scalp. 'Mr Quarrier is very particular about cleanliness, Jane. Next to Godliness he says, so mind you keep yourself clean. You will be well looked after here but you must do your bit.' Jane nodded dumbly, glad at least that this ordeal was over. She longed to tell John about it and wondered if he was out still in the cold streets or back at Auld Slowey's now: she would tell him everything when she saw him and hoped that would be soon.

Miss Mathieson then led Jane back along the cold corridor and down a stone staircase to a huge kitchen with a stove burning brightly, a worn wooden table and some stools. From a pantry she produced a chunk of bread, some cheese and a tin mug of milk. 'Make sure you finish this. There'll be nothing else till morning.' Jane ate and drank gratefully, wondering at her luck - *Maybe John was right about this place after all, but what will I have to do to earn my keep?* She remembered her father telling her, 'You'll get nothing for nothing in this world. You mark my words.'

2

John was making his way along the cold, dark streets with a heavy heart towards Auld Slowey's. He hoped he had done the right thing putting Jane into the orphanage, but it filled him with anxiety to think of her with strangers. He had hoped to visit her soon and see how she was settling, but Mr Galbraith had warned him to stay away for a while, saying she would 'adapt better to her new life' if she didn't have reminders of the past around her. *'What will her new life be?'* he wondered. With luck she would be fed and treated well and would remember that her family loved her, even if they couldn't care for her properly just now. He would get her back as soon as he was able: he would work hard with Auld Slowey and learn all there was to know about being a shoemaker; then he could make money for himself and Jane. What a lot of questions Mr Galbraith had asked about Jane and the family while he wrote everything down in a huge ledger. Who was alive? Who was dead? Where were those who were left?

John's head was spinning with trying to remember dates of birth and death. He had been relieved and proud that he was able to sign his name at the end of it to say he was agreeable to the Home looking after his sister. Mr Galbraith had asked what religion Jane was and if she attended church regularly; John told him the family were Roman Catholic but that since their parents had died they had not gone to church. Mr Galbraith said, 'No matter. She is still young enough to be saved.' If she could be saved from starvation and the dreaded Poorhouse at Barnhill, John would be happy. If there really was a god who was able to see into people's hearts, he would know that Jane was good and could do nothing about how her life had turned out. He remembered their mother, Roseanne, taking them all to Mass at Saint Mary's Church in Calton. It was a beautiful place, and Jane and their mother had loved the hymn-singing, but when Father Mooney had told them to pray for forgiveness for their sins in order to get into Heaven, John couldn't think what their sins were. His parents worked hard, but, like most people they knew, they had little money or food and often lived in great discomfort. Was it a sin to want more from life? Was that considered greed? It was true that after their parents had died, Ellen stole food for her family and was now being punished in Duke Street Prison, but what mother wouldn't be tempted to steal to save her starving children? Roseanne herself had known the loss of children; Peter first, aged four, from that dreadful disease, Consumption. Later, poor little Owen had gone into the Poorhouse with Roseanne at the age of two and had died in that horrible, damp and wicked place, surrounded by uncaring people.

Roseanne had come from Ireland as a young girl to escape the Great Famine which had brought starvation and death to thousands, and here in Glasgow she'd hoped to find a better life - for a time she had, but poverty brought a different kind of starvation and suffering. She often talked of Fermanagh in Ireland and how much better life had been there before the potato blight ruined crops and caused people to flee the country of their birth. She would sigh and say, 'We were poor there too, but we had room to breathe.' She had lived and worked on a farm: her family worked in the fields; the work was hard, but they had what food they could grow in the kitchen garden for themselves and they had beds to sleep in. The farmer who owned the land sold the crops they planted, tended and gathered in from the fields, but potatoes were plentiful and they were allowed to keep some, which supplemented their meagre wages. Roseanne would often recall, 'Your Granny Helen could make them 'pretties' into all sorts - hearty stews and soups and delicious potato bread. Makes my mouth water to think of it.' Life was hard but bearable. When the awful potato blight struck, their main source of food and employment disappeared.

They managed to get by for several months - but, one by one, the family left as work dried up and starvation threatened to kill them. Some went to England and some to Scotland. Roseanne spoke of the sea crossing which took most of the money she had. 'Hundreds of us crammed together, standing, like cattle.' All were hungry, and hope of a better future was the only comfort they had.

At the Broomielaw Docks in Glasgow they shuffled from the boat, weary and desperate. Glasgow seemed like a different world to Roseanne. 'It was dirty and noisy; the streets were full of people and there were more horses than I had ever seen in Ireland. I thought I'd never get used to it.' She had been given the name of someone from Fermanagh, a Mrs Kearney, who lived in the East End of Glasgow, but it took many hours to find her house. When, at last, she got there, Mrs Kearney opened the door and looked her over warily. 'I heard from my sister back home that you might come so I won't send you away, because God only knows where you'd end up, but I really don't have room for you. Come in for now and have some bread and tea.' She was kind and wanted to help, but could only offer Roseanne a floor to sleep on. Food was scarce here too. The potato blight had reached Scotland.

'You'll not find farm work because of that, but there are lots of factories you could try.'

Roseanne found work in a footwear factory in Bridgeton where the hours were long but she quickly learned how to bind boots to a high standard. She never saw daylight and this was depressing as the dark streets terrified her: tales of the 'penny gangs' who robbed people of even the smallest possessions made her run to Mrs Kearney's each night, frightened they might lunge out of the shadows to attack. She longed for Sundays when she could walk on Glasgow Green and amble along the banks of the Clyde, sit by the trees and imagine herself back in Fermanagh, on the shores of Lough Erne. It was on the Green that she met John's father, John Anderson - a shoemaker - and life seemed bearable again. She had recognised him from the factory where she worked and they got talking. She later told her children, 'With his twinkling eyes and dark hair he was so handsome that I soon lost my heart to him.' Like Roseanne, he had come to Glasgow seeking work, but he was from Dalkeith in Midlothian. His accent, different from Glaswegians, reminded her that they were both incomers and both striving for a better life. They had a lot in common. He was kind and loving, and soon they were married, full of hope again, in the beautiful Saint Mary's Church. They rented a room and kitchen in a large tenement building in Saltmarket and felt themselves lucky, as accommodation in this overcrowded city was hard to come by. 'We felt like royalty when we got it,' Roseanne used to say, laughing. 'That was before you lot made us poor again.'

Six children had been born to them in Glasgow over the years: Ellen, John, James, Jane, Peter and Owen. Their mother was no longer able to work but their father continued at his shoemaking trade, working late into the night in a corner of the kitchen after a day in the factory. 'It's just as well we live in a cold, wet country where rich people need shoes, but I wish I didn't need to make them all day, every day. I'm fair wabbit wi' it a'.' Roseanne was still mourning the loss of Peter when her husband became ill. Roseanne had gone to the 'Parish' to ask for help and had been sent to the Barony Poorhouse at Barnhill with the youngest children. Little Owen had not survived his stay there. Roseanne came home vowing to keep the rest of her children safe.

Ellen married young and James went to sea. John began to learn his trade as a shoemaker. He was proud to be called after his father and happy to follow in his footsteps. He still used the old shoemaking tools – a last, an awl and pincers - that Da had used, and thought of him often as he handled them. John lived with his master, Auld Slowey, becoming a lobby dosser while he was apprenticed. 'You can sleep in the lobby outside the workshop with the other boys learning their trade,' explained Auld Slowey. 'I won't charge you rent and you'll always be on time for work, so it'll suit us both.' John's employment might have helped the family eventually, but his mother seemed to have lost the will to live after her husband's death. At his funeral, she wept, 'Who would have thought my darling would end up in a pauper's grave? Nothing worse can happen to me now.' She had died, defeated by the disappointments in her life, at the age of 38.

John and Jane were heartbroken. The owner of the building put Jane out, saying, 'I'm sorry for your loss but I need to find another tenant who can pay the rent.' She was sent, once again, to the Barony Poorhouse till Ellen came and fought to take her to live with her. For a time it had seemed she would be safe, but Ellen's imprisonment had put an end to that.

John arrived at Schipka Pass, his head swimming with thoughts of his family. He climbed the covered path, holding onto the iron railings, passing people huddled on the ground there, seeking what shelter there was in the Pass. He had been told that Schipka Pass had been named after the site of a famous battle, fought on the other side of the world. The Russian Empire fighting the Ottoman Empire for supremacy. Britain supporting the Ottomans for its own ends. Thousands slaughtered along the way. *'Nothing much to celebrate in that name,'* thought John. *'More of a curse.'* Poor people with no homes to go to were battling here to survive.

When John reached Auld Slowey's door, he stepped into the lobby where several other boys were seated or lying on the floor. It was cold, but better than being outside, and John was grateful for the space left for him to sleep in. The door to the house opened and the Sloweys' servant, Theresa, came out. 'I thought I heard you come in. You've missed supper, but I'll find you something.' She disappeared, returning minutes later with some bread and a tin cup of milky tea. The bread was stale and hard, but breakfast was a long way off and it was more than those poor souls outside could hope for. He hoped Jane had been given something; couldn't bear to think of her hungry and alone. He prayed Mr Galbraith's promise to look after Jane would be kept.

3

In the warm kitchen at the Orphan Home, Jane finished the welcome supper and felt stronger for it. For the first time that day she thought life might be taking a turn for the better. *'I will work hard here to earn this food and these clothes. Whatever happens, I must try not to be sad. John will come back for me as soon as he can'*, she determined.

From somewhere in the building, she heard a clock chiming. Nine. She had learned to count with her father, laying out the laces, buckles, buttons and studs for the shoes and boots he made. The finished ones were counted and put aside to go to the factory and to be sold. She imagined she could still smell the leather and glue her father had used. Interrupting these thoughts, Miss Mathieson said quietly, 'Come, Jane, you must go to bed now. Remember the other children are already sleeping so get ready quietly. You will meet them all tomorrow.' Miss Mathieson led Jane along the cold corridor and up the stone staircase to the hall where she and John had first come into the Home. Then they climbed a curved wooden staircase which was highly polished and gleamed in the light of candles set in the walls. On and on, it seemed forever, till they reached a door with a sign - 'Girls' Dormitory 1'. *'What can this be?'* wondered Jane.

Miss Mathieson turned a large key in the lock and, as the heavy door swung open, Jane could see dimly, in the candlelight from the landing, three long rows of beds with iron frames, stretching along two sides and along the middle of the huge room. In each, she could make out a crumpled heap of covers and on each small pillow a head. She heard snuffling and snoring and, from one faraway corner, a whimper.

The bed nearest the door was empty and Miss Mathieson pointed to it. On it was laid a cotton gown. 'Put that on to sleep with and put your clothes back on in the morning. You must fold them neatly and place them over the rail at the foot of your bed. There is no water closet in here but use that bucket in the corner if you need to - we don't want any wet beds to clean. Be sure to replace the lid when you have finished. Go to sleep quickly, as you will be rising early in the morning.' Jane could not believe she was to have a bed to herself. *What other wonders could this Home hold?* In the bed, the sheet of rough fabric scratched her chin as she covered her shoulders. Miss Mathieson left, saying, 'Don't forget your prayers. Thank God for the mercy you have been shown and pray you can show your gratitude.' Jane heard the key being turned in the lock and wondered why the door was being locked. *Was it to protect them from thieves in the night?* Jane tightly closed her eyes, trying to pretend she was at home surrounded by her family. Soon she was asleep.

* * * * *

Jane's eyelids fluttered as she became aware of unfamiliar noises around her - whispering, rustling, footsteps. She struggled to wake and then remembered where she was. The huge room looked different with the daylight flooding in from windows set high in the walls. In beds all around were girls: some still asleep; others sitting up; some starting to dress. There was a queue of girls waiting at the bucket in the corner of the room. Judging by the smell, it had already been well used. Jane clutched the bedcovers around her, unsure of what to do next.

'Are you new?' The low voice came from the next bed where Jane saw a head of tousled red curls.

'What's your name?'

'Jane. I came last night.'

'I'm Kate. I've been here for ages. Are you an orphan?'

'Yes, whispered Jane, 'but my big brother or sister will be taking me back soon.'

'You're lucky', said Kate. 'I haven't got any brothers or sisters.' She looked sad and Jane felt a little guilty. Just then, the clock Jane had heard the night before chimed seven. Immediately, the key was heard turning in the lock and Miss Mathieson came in. She clapped her hands together several times and called out, 'Everyone up now. The middle row will wash first today. Don't waste time in idle chatter.' She walked quickly between the rows of beds, shaking girls awake as she went. Kate got up and stood beside Jane's bed.

'You can come with me if you want and I'll show you what you have to do.' Jane felt bewildered, and gratefully got out of bed to follow Kate along the landing to the bathroom. 'We only have a few minutes to wash in the morning, then we need to go back to the dormitory and put our clothes on. We have a bath once a week.' Jane copied Kate, washing her hands, face and neck. The girl's red hair reminded her of Ellen. Jane, with her straight brown hair had always envied Ellen's fiery curls.

Back in the dormitory, Jane dressed in the clothes she had been given the night before, noticing that all the other girls seemed to have the same clothes. They still felt strange and she was glad to put her own shoes on. They at least reminded her of her family. She saw the others tidying the covers on their beds and did the same. Nightdresses were folded and put under pillows. The girls began to line up at the door.

'What happens now?' Jane asked Kate. Kate put her fingers to her lips to silence Jane, but whispered,

'We get breakfast, then school. Wheesht the now.'

Jane's heart pounded. She had been to school sometimes in the church hall, but not since her mother had died. She wondered if the work would be difficult. *What if she couldn't do it? Would they make her leave?* As the last row of girls finished dressing, Miss Mathieson returned. 'Single file to the dining-room, girls, and no talking.'

Jane stayed close to Kate and they joined the long procession of silent girls downstairs. They entered the dining-room, a large room full of long tables and wooden stools. At one end stood two women wearing aprons; one gave each child a bowl of something as she passed and the other poured milk into each bowl. Jane recognised the smell of hot porridge and her mouth watered in anticipation. She took her bowl and sat beside Kate. When everyone was seated, the two women gave out pieces of bread and tin mugs of milk. It seemed like a feast to Jane. She longed to eat and drink and ask about school, but no-one else was moving or talking. Suddenly, at the far end of the room, Miss Mathieson rapped on a table with a spoon and called out, 'Grace.' Every head in the room was bowed. Every pair of hands was clasped. Every eye was closed.

'For what we are about to receive, may the Lord make us truly thankful'

'Amen' they all answered, and Jane copied them. There was then a clamour of voices as Miss Mathieson left them to eat their breakfast. Kate explained,

'We're not allowed to talk till after morning Grace, but we can talk now till it's time for school at 9 o'clock. I wonder what class you'll be in. What age are you?'

'Seven, but I haven't been to school for a long time.'

'I think I'm seven, so you might be in my class.' Jane hoped so. She ate and drank, savouring each mouthful.

After breakfast, Kate took Jane downstairs and outside to a large yard behind the Home, surrounded by a high stone wall. There, girls were in groups, talking or playing games. She learned that when Kate's parents had died, she, like Jane, had been in the Poorhouse before being brought to the orphanage.

'How long have you been here, Kate?'

'I'm not sure, but it seems like a long time.'

'Would you ever leave?'

'We can't leave. We're always locked in. Anyway, I don't have anywhere to go and it's better than being on the street.' Jane was glad she had a family who wanted her - but wondered how long she would have to wait for them to come for her.

4

A bell began to sound across the yard. A tall man dressed all in black stood ringing it at the door of a long, low building. Girls ran from all over the yard to stand in lines in front of it.

'That's Reverend Millar. He's my teacher. We'll ask him where you have to go.' Kate led her across the yard and stood before Reverend Millar.

'This is Jane. She's new.'

'Miss Mathieson has told me about you, Jane. You will be in the Junior class for the moment. Go in with Kate and we will see how you get on. Kate, take her with you.' Girls were moving quickly from the yard into the low building, then into several large rooms.

In the classroom, Jane recognised some girls from the dormitory or from breakfast. They all seemed to know what to do. They were arranging stools at desks and collecting slates and chalks from boxes in the corner, chatting as they went. Jane wished she could feel part of it all. As Reverend Millar entered, everyone fell silent and stood behind stools. He pointed to an empty stool in the front row. 'Stand there, Jane.' It seemed that every eye was on her as she moved behind it. Kate was several rows away but smiled at her, making Jane feel slightly reassured. 'Let us begin the day with The Lord's Prayer.' Clasping their hands in front of them, the girls began, 'Our Father, which art in Heaven...' Jane felt relieved that she recognised this and joined in. For some reason, the prayer was different at certain points from the one she had learned at Mass and she stumbled a little over these parts. She glanced up and saw Reverend Millar watching her closely: she felt herself blush. At the end of the prayer, Reverend Millar said, 'May the Lord bless our learning today and the work we are about to do.' The girls added 'Amen' and sat down at a hand signal from the Reverend. He handed Jane a slate and a chalk.

The first lesson was spelling and Reverend Millar called out letters and words for the girls to write down. Jane managed most of them. She had enjoyed learning to spell when she'd been attending school and still felt excited when she recognised words and understood their meaning. At home, her brothers and sister had helped her. Their parents could not read or write, but really wanted their children to learn. She could still hear Da's voice saying, 'Your lives will be better than ours if you can read and write. It'll give you power.' *Maybe staying in the orphanage for a while would be good for her. She would learn all she could, and if Ma and Da were watching from Heaven they would be proud of her.*

The next lesson was sums. Jane was less enthusiastic about these, but again she managed most of them. When Reverend Millar looked over the answers on her slate, he nodded and said, 'Well done, Jane. Good work.' Jane blushed again, this time with pleasure. The morning passed quickly and Jane got to know the names of some of the girls. When they were told to clean their slates with rags placed on their desks and put them away, Reverend Millar went out to the yard and rang the hand bell. Girls from all the classes went out into the yard, chattering noisily. Jane kept Kate's red curls in view and caught up with her in the yard.

'What happens now?

'Dinner. It's usually broth.'

'Why are there no boys, Kate?'

'They go to another orphan home across the River Clyde. Some girls have brothers that they haven't seen since they came here.'

'I haven't seen my brother James for a long time: he's on a ship at sea, but one day he'll be home. Our brother John will tell him where I am.' She didn't mention Ellen in prison.

The girls moved forward into the dining room and Jane sat beside Kate again. Other girls from the Junior class sat at the same table, asking

Jane about herself. When she explained how she was only here for a while, how her family would take her out as soon as they could, a pale-looking girl said, 'I thought my sister was coming for me, but I think she forgot.' Jane was sad for her but knew that John and Ellen would not, could not, forget about her.

At a noise from the front of the room, silence fell. Miss Mathieson once again led the Grace. Jane called out 'Amen' as loudly as the others and felt a little more part of things. Broth and bread were distributed; mugs of milk followed. *'How can I pay for all of this? Will John have to pay for it when he takes me out?'* she wondered. When dinner was over, the girls cleared away their plates and mugs, putting them on a large stand near the door. Miss Mathieson called out,

'Leviticus Group on kitchen duty. Everyone else outside. Jane Anderson, you will join Leviticus Group with Kate.'

'What's Leviticus?'

'It's the name of a book in the Bible, Jane. You'll soon know all of them', laughed Kate. She then showed Jane how to pile the plates and mugs on large tin trays. 'Not too heavy, mind. You don't want to drop them.' The trays were carried to the kitchen, where the dishes were washed in large tubs by some girls and laid out for the others to dry. They were then put in large cupboards, ready for the next meal. When everything was tidy, the girls went back outside.

The next hour was spent walking around the yard or playing games which involved skipping, jumping or running. Jane watched closely, trying to join in. Kate and the pale girl, Lizzie, stayed with her, answering her questions about the Home as best they could, but they didn't seem to know how long people stayed there or when their families visited. Lizzie said, 'We're part of the Quarriers family now - that's what they tell us.' Jane felt a knot of anxiety in her stomach but thought again about John's promise to come back for her. She must just be patient.

5

When the bell rang again, the girls went back inside, this time to sewing rooms. A middle-aged woman with grey hair held in a tight bun ushered the Junior class in. She smiled.

'Hello, are you Jane?'

'Yes, Miss'.

'Welcome. I am Mrs Walker. We're making napkins at the moment. Let's choose what you need.' Pieces of material and threads of bright colours were laid out on the desk. Jane was given a square of light material and allowed to choose two coloured lengths of thread, a blue that reminded her of the summer sky, and a green like grass. *'When I'm sewing, I'll think about being outside, walking on the Green with Ma',* she thought. Mrs Walker took her to a table, showed her how to fold the edges of the material and threaded a needle for her. 'You must use nice, neat stitches of the same length round all the edges. Our napkins are used by important visitors and we want them to be pleased with your work.' She did a few stitches for Jane, then gave her the needle to continue. Jane looked around the room at all the other girls who seemed to be working intently at their napkins. Mrs Walker was checking them as she walked around the room. Jane hesitantly pushed the needle through the fabric, catching her finger on its point where she was gripping the fold. Horrified, she saw blood and quickly sucked her finger to stop the bleeding. She then pressed it against her tunic, afraid of getting blood on the napkin. When the bleeding stopped, she tried again. It seemed impossible to hold everything at the same time and make nice stitches. Her finger throbbed. Mrs Walker came back to check on her. She showed her how to hold the material and avoid pricking her finger. After a few attempts, Jane mastered this, but, try as she might, she could not make neat stitches of the same length. 'Don't worry. Practice makes perfect', Mrs Walker smiled. 'Just keep going.' At the end of the lesson, Mrs Walker pinned a piece of paper with Jane's name on it to the now crumpled napkin and she put it in the box with everyone else's. Kate came over to join her.

'I'll never be able to do that', said Jane, on the verge of tears.

'Don't worry. We were all like that to start with', laughed Kate, and this made Jane feel better.

As they reached the yard outside, a tall man approached them.

'Are you Jane Anderson?' Jane nodded nervously.

'I'm Doctor Matthews. You must come to the infirmary with me.' Jane felt panic as she remembered the infirmary in the Poorhouse, full of children coughing or covered in sores: she could remember their awful cries. Some of them never came back out alive: their bodies were taken away on a cart. She thought of her brother Owen who had died in there and how her mother had cried every time she spoke of him.

'But I'm not sick, Sir.'

'That's what we want to check, Jane. We want to keep you in good health.' She followed him into the building, going up stairs and along corridors till they came to a room marked 'Surgery – Dr. Matthews'. Across the corridor was a ward with rows of beds, but only a few girls were in them. A nurse in a white uniform was giving someone a drink and everything looked clean.

In the surgery, Jane was told to take off her dress. Doctor Matthews looked in her eyes, her ears and her mouth. Some of her teeth were brown and broken but new ones had begun to grow in. The doctor put a cold, steel tube against her chest and back, listening through its other end.

'Now take deep breaths, Jane. Any pain?'

'No, Sir.' He told her to lift her petticoat and as she looked over his head in embarrassment, he prodded her stomach. It was uncomfortable but not sore. Her feet were examined before she was told to walk up and down the room. Her height was checked against a chart on the wall.

'You are small for your age, Jane, but your health is not bad. You must eat everything that you are given, exercise every day and keep yourself clean. Now you may put your dress back on and go back to the yard. I will walk with you.' He led her back through the building, then outside into the yard where the other girls were walking around or chatting. She looked for Kate's red hair and hurried to join her. She needed to go to the toilet and asked Kate where she should go. Kate pointed to a queue of girls waiting outside a stone shed. She joined them and when her turn came she gladly used the bucket; it was positioned under a wooden plank with a hole in it. She had to jump up to sit on the plank and hold on tight so that she didn't fall through. As she was leaving the shed, an older girl came in and pointed to a spigot on the wall. 'We have to wash our hands when we use the toilet.'

Back outside, girls were walking round the edge of the yard. In the centre, a tall girl called out instructions. 'March. Stop. Stamp your feet. March. Swing your arms. Keep going.' Jane joined in, and after a few minutes felt warm despite the cold afternoon. Just as a shower of rain began, the bell rang and the girls went inside to the dining-room.

'Why were we doing that?'

'We have to keep healthy so that we'll be able to work, and in case we're adopted'

'What does that mean?'

'Sometimes, people take children from here and keep them as their own. They don't want children who are weak or sick.' As Jane thought about this strange idea, Miss Mathieson entered. 'Silence for Grace.' Jane bent her head like the others, clasped her hands and closed her eyes. This time, she remembered more of the Grace than before.

After tea, Jane followed Lizzie and Kate to the large kitchen, carrying the tin trays of bowls from the tables. Lizzie showed her how to put them in piles. 'Four's enough so they don't fall over. And be careful not to drop any - they don't like things getting broken.' Back and forth they went between dining-hall and kitchen with what seemed like an endless number of bowls, cups and spoons. 'I like washing things best 'cause the water's lovely and warm, but it's not our turn', said Lizzie. 'The Seniors are lucky. They get to wash clothes. I'd like to do that.'

When all the dishes and spoons had been taken to the kitchen, the tables had to be wiped with wet cloths and the floors swept with brooms as tall as Jane. Her arms began to ache but she kept going under the watchful eye of Miss Mathieson who supervised everything the girls were doing, pointing out any stray crumbs they had missed. 'We don't want vermin here, do we?' she called loudly. Jane thought of the mice in her old home, appearing from holes in the walls, and the rats running around in the back court. She hated them and remembered the fear of crossing the back court in the dark to go to the lavatory, the terror that the scurrying, scrabbling creatures would touch her feet or worse. *No, she didn't want vermin here.* She brushed the floor with renewed purpose. At last Miss Mathieson was satisfied. 'Thank you, girls. Good work. You may go out to the yard now for some exercise.' Jane felt she had exercised enough already but followed the others back outside. There, girls were walking around in twos and threes, round and round the edge of the yard, beside the high walls.

'We have to keep healthy and busy', said Lizzie. 'Reverend Millar says the Devil finds work for idle hands.' She gave a heavy sigh.

'Do you ever go outside the walls? asked Jane, already feeling that the world she had known had disappeared.

'We go to church on Sundays, but Mr Quarrier says he's going to build us a village with gardens to play in. Don't know when that will be, but I wish it could be soon.' Kate joined in. 'Mr Quarrier has found a place in the countryside, far away from here. We're going to live in houses and play in gardens and go to school.' Her brown eyes sparkled. 'That'll be wonderful, won't it?' Jane couldn't imagine it, never having been out of Glasgow, but thought about the freedom of running around on Glasgow Green. *Mr Quarrier must be very rich.*

The bell interrupted and the girls lined up at the door. Miss Mathieson led them along a corridor and into a large hall where they sat in rows. Reverend Millar stood at a wooden stand on which lay a huge book.

'Is he going to tell us a story?' asked Jane.

'Sort of', laughed Kate. 'He reads to us from the Bible - the story of the Lord.' She raised her eyebrows mischievously, smiling.

'Today you will hear about the Good Samaritan who helped someone that many others had passed by. Think how you have a Good Samaritan in Mr Quarrier and how he has helped you in your time of need.' Jane listened as he read aloud and wondered if she was really like the poor person in the story.

'Bow your heads now and we will thank God that you have been saved from the lives you once led. We will thank Him for the shelter and food you receive, and pray that you can repay Him by leading a good life according to His commandments.' Jane was confused about who to thank. At the end of Reverend Millar's prayer, she called out 'Amen' with the others, but looked forward to asking what John and Ellen thought of it all.

When prayers were over, the girls filed out and went to the dining-hall where cups of milk were laid out. Each girl took one, drank the milk then took her cup to the kitchen. 'We have to get washed now and go to bed,' said Kate. Again they took turns in the lavatories and bathroom before going to the dormitory. Jane folded her clothes, put on her nightgown, then slid under the covers. When Miss Mathieson came and said, 'Silence now and go to sleep', she felt suddenly tired. She thought of Ma who used to cuddle her at bedtime. Tears stung her eyes, but she told herself, *'I'm lucky to be here – lucky to have a bed and food to eat and clothes to wear, but I want to be in the outside world again with my family. They'll be amazed to hear what goes on in the Home.'*

6

As the days passed, Jane became more familiar with the people around her and the things she had to do. Clothes were changed on Saturday.

'I've only had them on for a few days. They're still clean', Jane protested to Lizzie as they dressed.

'We have to follow all the rules, Jane. Saturday is changeover day for everybody and everything.' Miss Mathieson came looking for Jane just then. 'Come with me. You need to be fitted for boots, and a cape and bonnet for church tomorrow.' In a musty-smelling room, brown boots of various sizes were lined along shelves on the wall. Brown capes hung on hooks all around. Miss Mathieson took down several pairs of boots and tried them beside Jane's feet for size. Then she said,

'These should do. Put them on and I will dispose of your old shoes.'

'Please, Miss, can I keep my shoes? My brother made them for me.'

'No, Jane. They are old and dirty. Boots will be better for you. And look after them - someone else may need them when you outgrow them.' Jane's heart sank as she watched Miss Mathieson drop her shoes in a basket, feeling another part of her life was disappearing. A brown cape was selected for Jane; cotton bonnets were tried on till one was found to fit. Miss Mathieson led her to a cloakroom where she pointed to a peg with a card marked 'Jane Anderson'.

'Your name will be put on your cape and bonnet and you will find them here tomorrow before Church. You must always return them to your peg. Now join the others in the Hall till dinner-time.'

'Thank you, Miss.'

Back in the Hall, Jane's group were chatting or reading books at the tables set out around the edge of the room. Jane spotted Kate and went to join her at a big table. Lizzie was there and another girl who had fair hair, and freckles across her nose and cheeks. Jane remembered her mother calling the golden marks angel kisses. James had them.

'This is Tilly,' said Lizzie.

'My real name's Matilda, but nobody calls me that anymore. My stepfather did but he's dead, thank the Lord.' She smiled and Jane saw gaps where teeth should have been. Her tongue moved instinctively to her own gaps, thankful they were at the back.

'Why are you glad he's dead?'

'Because he used to get drunk and beat my mother and make her cry. When she died, he put me out on the street every day to beg. If I didn't take him enough money to buy drink, he beat me. He used to say he would sell me if I didn't do better. I hated him. One night he didn't come home, and the next day the old woman next door came and told me he'd been found dead in the street. She brought me here and now I'm happy.' The dinner bell rang and Tilly got down awkwardly from her seat. She began to walk away and Jane noticed how she limped as if one leg was shorter than the other.

'Is she alright?' Jane asked Kate.

'She's fine, but she's got something called Pals ...Prals...Paralysis, that's it. She doesn't like when people notice, so don't say anything.' Jane rushed to line up, looking forward to warm broth. Regular food was still a wonder and she gratefully ate whatever she was given. Now when she said Grace, she really meant it and prayed she'd never go hungry again. *If only Ellen and her children could be so lucky.*

In the afternoon, the girls were called to the Hall where Reverend Millar stood at his podium, looking stern. The girls filed into rows of seats. On each one was a small leather-bound book. Jane tried to read the word on the cover. 'Hymnal'.

'What's this?' she asked Kate.

32

'It's the words of hymns, songs we have to sing in church tomorrow. We need to practise them so that we'll sing well in church.' Reverend Millar called for silence then said,

'We will begin with Psalm 42, *The Lord's My Shepherd*. Turn to page 14. All stand.' As pages were rustled and feet shuffled, Jane was aware of music starting up, and noticed a piano in the corner of the room. A woman wearing a hat with a large feather sat on a stool, playing some notes while the girls found the correct page.

'Now, after three; one, two, three.' The pianist began to play and the girls joined in. Jane tried to read the words as they sang, and moved her lips. She wished she knew the tune - it sounded lovely. Hopefully, she would soon learn.

After practising many hymns, some more than once, Reverend Millar seemed satisfied. 'Now,' he said, 'I have an announcement to make. Tomorrow in church we will be joined by a very special visitor - Mr Quarrier himself. I want you all to sing out as loudly and beautifully as you can. Remember you are in Mr Quarrier's care here and have many reasons to be grateful to him. Let's make him proud of you. Now go quietly into the yard till tea is ready.'

After tea, the girls were left to read, chat or walk in the yard. Bedtime arrived and Jane climbed gladly into bed. As usual, she thought of her family, imagining each face in turn, ones she would never see again and ones she longed to see. She tried not to cry, but quiet tears slid down her face in the dark.

7

Next morning the girls practised their hymn-singing once more. Already, Jane felt the tunes were more familiar and she could hear them in her head even after the girls had left the hall to go and get ready for church.

'Where's the church?' Jane asked Kate as they once more washed hands and faces.

'Just next to the Home, not far to walk.' They went to the cloakroom where Jane found her peg, and Kate helped her put on her cape and bonnet. They felt strange. She had never had a hat but remembered being held under her ma's woollen shawl if the weather was bad. After Ma died, Jane kept the shawl and used it herself. In the Poorhouse it went missing and she never saw it again. 'Line up in the yard, girls. Juniors at the front; Seniors behind.' Jane followed the others and joined the long line against the high wall. She shivered with nerves, but was looking forward to being outside of the Home for the first time since John had brought her here.

Reverend Millar arrived to lead them to church and Miss Mathieson followed on as they moved through the building and into the hallway where she and John had first arrived. Girls were walking through the open front door. Once outside, Jane could see the procession moving forward and then girls standing in line around a huge stone building. Jane could not believe she hadn't noticed it the night she arrived, but it had been dark and foggy then. The church seemed huge and very grand. Built of gold-coloured stone, it had gleaming windows stretched along its side walls. High up on the roof soared a huge steeple from which a bell rang out. On the front of the steeple was a large clock with golden numbers.

All around the church were grand houses and people walking towards the church, dressed in beautiful clothes and hats. Others were arriving in carriages pulled by horses. Passengers got down from their carriages and horses stamped their feet noisily, breathing clouds of steam into the cold air. Immediately the carriages moved away, a man darted forward from across the road, pushing a hand-cart. Quickly, he shovelled up the horses' dung into the cart then returned to where he had been waiting. The girls moved forward and up stone steps set between vast pillars at the front of the church. Inside, they were led to the upper floor where they sat in rows on long wooden seats. Jane could see down into the lower floor. More huge pillars seemed to hold the roof in place. Daylight poured in through the beautiful coloured-glass windows, and all around were highly-polished wooden seats and rails. People in the church were wearing clothes more lovely than any Jane had seen before. She remembered Saint Mary's which she had loved - it too was a beautiful building, but she thought of the people who had gone to Mass there. Their clothes seemed like rags by comparison to these. Beside her, Kate whispered, 'Look, Mr and Mrs Quarrier are here.' She pointed to a man and woman sitting in the front row downstairs. Jane had imagined that Mr Quarrier would look like a king because he owned the Home but instead he wore plain, dark clothes and had black hair and a beard. His wife wore a large hat with feathers, but her dress was also dark and plain. As they filed into their seats, beautiful music was being played by a man seated at an organ, high up in the gallery. Jane was engrossed in the whole spectacle. Kate nudged her and passed her a hymnal. 'Quick - page fourteen.'

The organ music stopped and downstairs everyone stood up holding hymnals; only the rustling of pages broke the silence. From a door at the front of the church a tall man entered who faced the congregation. 'Welcome, everyone, to Saint Andrew's Parish Church this fine morning. I am Reverend Thompson. Let us praise God by singing *The Lord's my Shepherd.'* The organ music began again and Reverend Millar led the girls in song. Their voices joined with those of the congregation and the church seemed to fill with the beautiful sound. Reverend Thompson read from the Bible and then introduced their benefactor.

'This morning, we have with us Mr William Quarrier whom many of you will know from his good works with the poor children of Glasgow. He would like to address you regarding this wonderful, on-going work. Mr Quarrier?'

'Thank you, Reverend Thompson, for allowing me to speak this morning. I know many of your dear congregation but not all. For those of you who do not know me, I hope to make you familiar with my work. Fourteen years ago, I was led by the Lord to help the poor children of our town who were increasing in number at an alarming rate. Due to poverty, disease and the death of their parents, thousands of these children were living in appalling conditions on our streets, many of them, indeed, drifting into the similarly increasing criminal ranks to survive. Knowing the dangers of poverty, I wanted to help them. I began, with the help of family and friends, to train the boys to work, some as shoemakers like myself. This led to the shoe-black brigade, children being paid for honest work on the streets. The girls were taught housekeeping skills. With continuing support, these children were also fed and taught to read and write. They attended Sabbath Schools to learn the word of God. Seven years ago, we opened our first Children's Home in Glasgow. We now have several, all full at all times. Many of our children are adopted into good families; others old enough to work can leave and do so, but always there are others to take their places.' Around the room, members of the congregation listened intently, raising their eyebrows at spouses and nodding.

'Two years ago, thanks to generous subscriptions, I was able to buy farmland near Bridge of Weir in Renfrewshire. To date, we have six large houses built there. My vision is to send children from our Homes to live in smaller groups like families, in a place where they can continue to be trained for work but also enjoy the open air and thrive in a healthy, happy community. Soon, with the completion of building work, we hope our Orphan Cottage Homes will be worthy of that name. You, dear brothers and sisters in God, can help. Together we must lessen the evil of our world. This year, our organisation has raised almost eight thousand pounds from generous benefactors. Donations have ranged from one shilling from a local grandmother to one hundred pounds from an anonymous friend. Every penny has been put to good use. Anything you can spare will be gratefully received. Think of the lives these poor, degraded children live compared to yours. Remember what Jesus said, "Inasmuch as ye have done it unto the least of these, ye have done it unto Me." Just as we ask in The Lord's Prayer, "Give us each day our daily bread", I now ask you to help me provide the same for them. In this beautiful church, built by past generations of Glasgow merchants, please let your heart be moved. Look at our girls, here this morning from the nearby City Orphan Home (at this, he pointed to the gallery). They are well-fed and clothed and singing the praises of the Lord in fine voice. Let us make this possible for as many others as we can.'

Mr Quarrier sat down again and many people were looking up at the girls as if, perhaps, noticing them for the first time. Jane was glad to be wearing her new clothes. Reverend Thompson moved again to the front of the church. 'Thank you Mr Quarrier. Long may your marvellous work continue. With God's help, and the generosity of our brothers and sisters, I know it will. Let us stand and sing our final hymn for today, *Abide with Me.*' The organist played some introductory notes; then the church filled again with the sound of singing. As the hymn finished, people began to leave the church. Miss Mathieson led the girls back to the Home. 'Well done, girls. Now go and hang up your bonnets and capes, then go for dinner.'

The girls chattered as they went, excited at the prospect of a new Home in the country. Jane tried to join in, but inwardly she felt anxious. *Will John or Ellen be able to find me there? What if they can't?* At dinner, she asked Kate,

'How can I let John know that we might be moving from here? I want him to know where I'm going so that he can find me.'

'I don't know. I don't have anyone to tell. You could ask Reverend Millar.' All day, Jane thought about this. She didn't want to make any trouble, but couldn't bear the thought of losing touch with her family. At evening prayers, she prayed for courage. Afterwards, she approached Reverend Millar. She hesitated momentarily, imagining his possible anger - but knew she had to try, whatever happened.

'Please, Sir, if we move to the country will someone tell my family where I am?' She could not stop her lip from trembling. The minister seemed to think for a moment, then said,

'I'm sure Mr Galbraith will know how to contact them. Why don't I help you write a note for them and he can send it?' Jane nodded, relieved. Reverend Millar went to a desk and took a piece of paper, pen and ink from a drawer.

'To whom are you writing?'

'My brother, John Anderson, please.' She watched as he wrote a few lines in beautiful but complicated writing.

'Here, Jane. I have explained to John what might happen and how he can find you. Can you sign your own name at the bottom of the note?' He handed her the pen and she carefully wrote her name, glad she was able to do this at least. Finally, he pressed on the page with blotting paper, folded it and put it in his pocket.

'Off you go now, Jane. Do not worry anymore.'

'Thank you, Sir,' she sighed. When Jane had gone, Reverend Millar made his way to Mr Galbraith's study. He knocked on the door and entered. Mr Galbraith was seated at his desk with piles of papers in front of him. Behind him, a fire blazed in the hearth.

'Good evening, Reverend. As you can see, we have already had some responses to Mr Quarrier's appeal for support for the Cottage Homes project. Many parishioners have pledged large amounts of money.'

'That is very heartening, Mr Galbraith. He will be delighted. On the same subject, young Jane Anderson is anxious for her family to know where she might be going. I have written a note for her, to be sent to her brother.' He passed the note to Mr Galbraith, who raised his eyebrows and said,

'Indeed? Unexpectedly fine feelings for one so young and in her situation. Thank you for your help, Reverend. I will deal with this, but you must excuse me now. I have much work to do here.'

'Of course.' Reverend Millar left the room, thankful that Jane's problem was resolved. At his desk, Mr Galbraith re-read the note, sighed and shook his head. 'Ungrateful wretch.' He threw the note on the fire. In seconds it had disappeared, and he turned back to his work.

8

Almost a month had passed since John had put Jane into the Orphan Home. He was relieved to think she had a safe roof over her head and food to eat but he also desperately wanted to see her; hear how she was. He remembered how she'd clung to him before she was taken away. *Please let her be alright.* Mr Galbraith had warned him not to visit her too soon, to allow her to 'settle' - but maybe he could ask at the door how she was. Surely they wouldn't mind that. The next day was Sunday when he didn't work so he would go then. He tossed and turned during the night, anxious to put his plan into action. When he rose, he washed carefully, trying to look tidy, while still wearing the clothes in which he had slept. Theresa called from the kitchen, 'Breakfast.' With the other apprentices, he hungrily ate the bread and drank the milk provided by his master, then set off.

As he walked out of Schipka Pass, he heard his name being called. He turned to see a young man in uniform approaching. 'John - It's me, James.' John had not seen his brother since he had been sent to HMS Cumberland to train as a sailor. He had been a pale, freckly boy of 11 then. Now he looked like a man; he was tall and broad-shouldered, with the ruddy complexion of someone who worked in the open air.

'James, I cannae believe it. How are ye?'

'I'm feeling strange, John. I heard about Ma dying, but when I got the message they told me it wouldn't do any good to come home as the funeral was over. Now my training's finished and I'll be going to sea, but I just wanted to see you all first. I went to our house but other people live there now. Then I went to Ellen's, and Henry told me what happened to her. He let me spend the night and told me where to find you. Where's Jane?'

'She's in the Orphan Home in James Morrison Street. I was feart she would have to go back to the Poorhouse after Ellen was jailed. They've said she'll be well looked after, and that I shouldn't visit too soon, but I'm worried in case she hasn't settled. I'm going there now. Come with me. Jane will be really happy to see you - she missed you when you left.'

'I missed you all, but I wasn't allowed to come home because of why I got sent there. I tried to write a letter home but couldn't write the words I wanted to say. My own fault, I know. When I should have been learning to read and write I was on the streets getting into trouble. I know I wasn't a good boy after Da died and Ma was ill. I wanted to say sorry to Ma, but I thought if I finished the training and got a job, she'd be proud of me after all. It was maybe for the best that the police stopped me from getting into any more trouble on the streets. The training on the ship was hard but now it's over and I'm able to get a real job at sea. It wasn't what I thought I'd be doing, but I think I'll have a good life now.'

'Ma would have been proud of you, James; Da too. All they ever wanted was for us to have a better life than them.'

'What about you? Will you stay wi' Auld Slowey?'

'My apprenticeship's nearly finished. Auld Slowey will give me my Journeyman papers soon. I could get a job somewhere else then, but he's asked me to stay on with him and train to be a Master Shoemaker like him. I'm thinking about that. I'll have wages as a Journeyman and could maybe take Jane out of the Orphan Home, but finding a place for us to live will be hard.' The brothers walked along, sharing stories of their lives apart, happy to be together again. Soon they reached James Morrison Street. John went to the door of the Home and knocked. It was opened by a young woman. She looked them over suspiciously.

'Can I help you?'

'Yes, please. I am John Anderson and my sister Jane was taken in here a few weeks ago. This is my brother James. We wondered how Jane's getting on.'

'I know Jane. She's well and happy, so dinnae worry about her.'

'Can we see her? My brother's been at sea and he's going away again. He'd dearly like to speak to her before he goes.'

'Sorry; that's not possible. The girls aren't allowed visitors. Anyway, she's not here. They're all at church.'

'What church?'

'I cannae tell ye that.' She looked nervously over her shoulder as footsteps sounded in the hallway.

'Margaret, who is at the door?'

'Jane Anderson's brothers, Mr Galbraith. They want to see her.' Mr Galbraith came to the door. Margaret curtsied and retreated into the shadows of the hallway.

'Good day, Mr Anderson. Jane is not here at present, as Margaret will have told you. However, if you remember, I said you shouldn't visit Jane for fear of unsettling her. Surely you don't want her upset after all the work that has gone into making her content here.'

'I would never wish to upset her, Sir. I am glad that she's well and happy, but my brother here has only a short time in Glasgow before he goes to sea. Could he not speak to her, please? I'm sure she'd want to see him.' Mr Galbraith looked at them with raised eyebrows.

'That would be completely against the rules of the Home, I'm afraid. You signed the papers to put Jane into our care and now you must let us do our job. I assume you still do not have a home for Jane to go to. Have you?'

'No, Sir.'

'In that case, please go now and do not return. I know you have Jane's welfare at heart, but rest assured so have we. You are creating a disturbance and I would not want to have you removed by the Constabulary. I will let Jane know that you enquired after her. I'm sure that will please her greatly.' Without further conversation, Mr Galbraith firmly closed the door.

'What have I done?' cried John anxiously.

'What you thought was for the best', replied James. 'They say she's well and happy and we must take comfort from that. Let's go before we're arrested.' James had no wish to be in the clutches of the police again, particularly now that he had a job waiting. As they moved away, James had an idea.

'What if we wait nearby till they come back from church and try to see her, at least? That would be better than nothing.'

'Aye, you're right, James. Let's find somewhere we won't be noticed.' They spied a shop doorway on the other side of the street and hurried to stand in it. As they waited, carriages began to arrive and stand in front of the large church facing them.

'Could Jane be in there, John?'

'It's certainly close to the Home, but I don't know where they go. I don't know that church either.' Just then, people started coming out of the building. They all seemed very grand. Some walked around the square and went into large stone houses there. Others came down the steps and climbed into waiting carriages to be driven off. The boys saw a minister shaking hands with people as they left. When it seemed no-one else was coming out, John noticed the woman who had taken charge of Jane in the Home, the night he had taken her there. She shook hands with the minister, went down the steps, then turned and waved her hand towards the doorway. At her signal, a long line of girls came outside. She crossed to the Orphan Home and they followed her in twos, passing in front of her at the door. 'It's them', whispered John. 'It must be.' John and James scanned each face in turn. James had not seen Jane for several years and was worried he might not recognise her. The line was disappearing quickly into the Home. Suddenly, John grasped his arm. 'Look, there she is, beside the wee red-haired girl.' Jane was holding the other girl's hand and they were smiling and talking. She looked well in her smart clothes and seemed very much part of the group. John longed to run across or call out to her, but almost as soon as they had seen her she went inside. Following the group was another minister, who seemed to the boys like a guard. James put an arm around John's shoulder.

'Well, at least we've seen her. She looks well and happy, as they said. I'm sure you've done the right thing, John. She would never be dressed like that with us.' John nodded, glad to have James's approval, but he felt a lump in his throat and struggled not to cry.

'Let's walk through the Green. I'd like to see it again before I go, and I have to sign on and board my new ship at the Broomielaw by 3 o'clock.' The brothers walked to nearby Glasgow Green, where they and their parents had spent many a happy hour. It was bustling with people enjoying their day of rest. Trees and flowers were in bloom and the sun was shining on the River Clyde. John's spirits lifted a little. He wanted to enjoy the time he had left with James before he too went to a new life.

'How long will you be away? Are you going far?'

'I don't rightly know, John, but many months I should think. The ship's picking up goods from here and other ports in England, but then we'll be sailing to France and on to America.'

'Try to stay in touch. Maybe someone could help you write to me. Even a note with your name on it will let me know you are safe and well. Use Auld Slowey's address at 21 Schipka Pass, and I'll leave word there if I move somewhere else.'

'I'll do that', promised James. He too felt better for seeing his brother and sister, and feeling part of a family again, whatever the future held.

They left the Green and walked along the Clydeside to Broomielaw, where their mother Roseanne had landed from Ireland many years before. The dockside was full of the hustle and bustle of ships being loaded and unloaded by dockyard workers, and passengers preparing to board. The noise of ships' horns blared over that of barrows being pushed over the cobbles; wagons clattering along iron tracks and the shouting of dockside workers and sailors. James pointed to a large sailing ship with three tall masts, berthed alongside the dock. 'That's my ship, the S.S. Kilkenzie. I have to see the Harbourmaster before I can go on board.' John waited while James went into a large shed nearby. He emerged some time later holding a sheet of paper in his hand and with a canvas bag slung over his shoulder. 'I've signed on, John. I must go aboard now.' The brothers hugged awkwardly, feeling suddenly shy at saying their farewells. John watched as James went up the long gangplank onto the ship. He turned and waved, then disappeared from view. Weary, and suddenly lonely, John made his way back to Auld Slowey's.

9

Weeks passed and Jane became more comfortable in her new surroundings. When she woke in the morning, she no longer had to remind herself of where she was. She knew many of the girls by name; knew where things were and what the daily routine was. Lessons and visits to church were enjoyable. *John and Ellen knew her situation and would come for her when they could. Then they would see what she had learned and let her help out at home, wherever that might be.* The Spring weather meant more time outdoors in the sunshine. She now looked forward to games in the yard and was able to join in the songs that were part of them.

One morning in late April, Miss Mathieson made an announcement. 'Mr Quarrier has asked me to tell you about a special visitor to our Home this week. We are very honoured to have Miss Bilbrough, a friend of Mr Quarrier who has come all the way from Canada to visit us. She has made the long journey by boat, especially to visit our Homes here in Glasgow. You will therefore be on your very best behaviour, and be polite if you are spoken to while she looks around. She is visiting the classrooms and she is dining here tomorrow evening, so some of you will be helping out in the dining room.' She then gave instructions to the various groups about their duties during the visit. As the girls filed out, Jane asked Kate,

'Where is Canada?'

'I don't know, but if she came by boat it must be on the other side of the Clyde.'

'I know my mother came from Ireland by boat, and that was a long journey, so maybe it's near there.'

'Maybe. We can ask Reverend Millar. I'm sure he knows everything.' In class, when lessons were over, Kate raised her hand.

'Yes, Kate?'

'Sir, Miss Mathieson says there's a visitor coming from Canada. Where is that?'

'A long way away, Kate. It is in the New World, in North America, and our visitor, Miss Bilbrough, will have crossed the Atlantic Ocean to get here. I will show you on the map.' From a cupboard, he produced a large coloured chart which he held up.

'This is a map of the world and here is Scotland.' He pointed to a small shape which looked to Jane like a cloak with a hood. 'And here is Canada.' This time, he pointed to a very large shape on the other side of a blue-coloured area which he said was the Atlantic Ocean.

'She has made a great journey to visit you so make it worth her while. Show her the good things you have learned here, so that she will know how you have improved through the goodness of God and his servant, Mr Quarrier. Now go to dinner and give grateful thanks for that. Remember there are many hungry children outside our walls who are as miserable as you once were.' Jane still could not imagine where Canada was, but remembered again what life had been like before she came to the Home. At dinner she enthusiastically joined in Grace.

Afterwards, Jane's group went to the large hall where they usually met for prayers and hymns. Miss Mathieson gave out brooms and dusters to the younger girls. Jane and Tilly dusted and polished the wooden panelling around the room while others swept the floor. The usual rows of chairs had been cleared away and in the middle of the floor stood a long wooden table. The kitchen maids who normally served the food in the dining-room were attending to this. They laid on it huge white table covers, making sure the edges were even all round. Twenty chairs were put in place around the table. Then trolleys were wheeled in, bearing gleaming cutlery. At each place, knives and forks and spoons were carefully arranged. Mrs Walker arrived with a box of napkins, freshly washed and pressed. Jane recognised the napkins they had been making in sewing class. Some older girls were shown how to place them beside the cutlery on the table. Next, the kitchen hands set out sparkling glasses and china cups and saucers. Jane had never seen anything so marvellous, and felt thrilled to have been part of the preparations, even though it had been tiring. Tilly seemed to be limping more than usual when they were dismissed.

'Is your leg very sore?' Jane asked.

'Yes, bending and kneeling's hard for me, but the doctor said I'll soon have a new boot which'll help.' Jane held onto her going downstairs, afraid she would fall over. She felt guilty for enjoying the preparations when it must have been hurting Tilly.

In the evening, the girls were taken again to the hall, where they practised singing hymns in preparation for Miss Bilbrough's visit. As they stood, repeating some of the hymns several times, Jane saw Tilly's lip tremble. 'Here, Tilly. Put your arm through mine and I'll hold you up.' On Tilly's other side, Kate put her arm around her waist. Lizzie stood behind her, ready to catch her if she were to fall back. At last, after what seemed like hours, the hymn-singing was over and they could go to bed. Before they left, Reverend Millar called out, 'Remember Miss Bilbrough in your prayers tonight. God willing, she will enjoy her visit and find you all as she would wish. We want her to be able to tell people in Canada good things about you.' As Jane lay in her bed, she prayed instead for Tilly, wishing her pain could be helped. She hoped God was listening and not too busy with the prayers for Miss Bilbrough.

10

William Quarrier stood on the steps of the Home, watching as the coachman opened the door of the carriage outside. As the woman passenger prepared to step down, he moved forward.

'Good morning. Miss Bilbrough?'

'I am she. You must be Mr Quarrier.' She put out her hand and Quarrier shook , then held her elbow to help her down. She held her long coat and dress up with one hand and the brim of her large hat with the other. He turned to the coachman. 'Take the lady's trunks to 318 St Vincent Street. My wife is waiting there for them.'

'Welcome to Glasgow, Miss Bilbrough. I trust your journey was not too onerous.'

'I confess it was difficult at times, but God's work is not always easy. We must simply do what is required of us. I'm happy to meet you at last.'

'We are honoured to have you here. Please come inside.' Along the hallway, Miss Mathieson and the house servants were lined up. Miss Bilbrough shook the hand of each. Quarrier turned to a housemaid. 'Bring tea to Mr Galbraith's study, please.' They entered the study where a fire blazed in the large fireplace and Mr Galbraith stepped forward.

'This is Mr Galbraith who runs this Home for us. He is in charge of all staff as well as the orphan girls. He ensures that everything runs smoothly and keeps me informed of all that happens. After tea, he will show you some of our records and explain our operation.'

'How do you do, Mr Galbraith?'

'I am well, thank you, and delighted to meet you. Please take a seat.' He indicated several chairs around a large oak table. Miss Bilbrough moved towards a chair at the window, squeezing between other chairs and the long curtains. Her hat caught on the velvet material and she quickly pulled it off and handed it to Mr Galbraith, laughing. 'I'm sure we can dispense with formality now.' They all laughed, relaxing.

'How busy this city is, gentlemen. On the way here from the ship, I was astonished by the number of people in the streets and the business being conducted all around. Glasgow seems like a very industrious place. However, I also noticed the condition of adults and children begging in the streets. There is no doubt that you are performing a very worthwhile service to your community. I hope I can assist you in your endeavours.' She turned to Quarrier.

'I'm sure when you visit Canada, you will see the advantages we offer. Who will accompany you?'

'My wife, Isabella, and our daughter, Agnes. Isabella is very involved in the Orphan Homes of Scotland, and I should like Agnes to be more involved in future. You will meet them both later.'

'I look forward very much to that.' Tea and freshly-baked bannocks in china dishes were brought in, and conversation lulled while the three of them enjoyed this treat. Mr Galbraith then pulled the cord on the wall to summon the maid, who smartly cleared the table. Mr Galbraith went to his desk and laid out several leather-bound ledgers. He explained to Miss Bilbrough that these were the records of girls taken in over the previous two years. He outlined their dire circumstances on arrival; many of them had been taken off the streets, where they were at risk of crime, disease, even death. This situation, he told her, was duplicated for the boys taken in. They were placed in separate Homes in the city.

'We are responsible for several hundred children at any time. We feed and clothe them, train them for future work and teach them the word of God. We cannot, however, keep them forever or guarantee them a good life when they leave us.'

'In that case,' said Miss Bilbrough, 'it is imperative that we take as many of them as possible to Canada. The children who have already gone are proving very acceptable to host families and have settled well. We receive requests on a daily basis for more.' She explained that, initially, her organisation had migrated mainly boys to work on farms, but now it was clear that girls would also be welcome, to fill jobs which could be performed by them on the land and in the homes of farming families. She suggested migrating a small number of girls the following month, with a view to increasing that number on subsequent trips. Quarrier tugged on his beard.

'That is certainly worth considering. We are already making preparations for forty boys to make the journey. Mr Galbraith, do you think we could have what twenty girls would need in time for the next sailing in May?'

'I will check what funds are available. All told, it costs £10 to send a child to Canada equipped with suitable clothing. At the moment, we probably have enough to purchase boots. The boys in the Cessnock home have some trunks they have already made in their workshops. I will check if there would be enough for the girls as well.' He suggested approaching the church groups who were working on making clothes for the boys and requesting additional clothing for girls. Mr Quarrier nodded vigorously.

'Excellent. Furthermore, when Miss Bilbrough addresses our guests this evening, telling them of the success of our scheme so far, I am sure they will be glad to help, even though time is short.' He explained that the guests would be prominent businessmen, many of whom had been generous in the past.

'In addition, we would then have places for twenty more girls here as a result, and that is surely desirable to all who have children's best interests at heart.'

'Splendid.' said Miss Bilbrough. She went on to outline how the running of the Child Migration Scheme was evolving in Canada. The Canadian Receiving Home, Marchmont House at Belleville, run by Miss Annie Macpherson, had previously taken children from throughout the British Isles, but very soon Miss Bilbrough would take charge of its running and take only Scottish children. Such was the interest in Canada in the Child Migration Scheme, that Miss Macpherson would be opening further distribution centres for children from other places.

'Sending girls on the next trip will allow us to assess the likelihood of success in that respect.'

'Indeed. It's fortuitous that my wife and daughter are going on that trip, as they will be better placed to assess and deal with any difficulties relating to the girls as they arise. Mr Galbraith, draw up a list of those girls who have been with us longest and have acquired the necessary skills for this exciting venture. In the meantime, Miss Bilbrough, would you care to see the girls on their everyday activities?'

'With pleasure.'

As they left the room, Mr Galbraith turned back to his ledgers with a sigh and drew his pen, ink and paper towards him.

11

In Reverend Millar's classroom, the girls were copying out spelling words when the door was opened by Mr Quarrier. 'Good morning, girls. Please stand up to greet our visitor, Miss Bilbrough!' They got to their feet and Miss Bilbrough stood before them - smiling, but her eyes seemed to search every corner of the room.

'Good morning, girls. I'm glad to meet you and see you working so hard.'

'Good morning, Miss!' they chorused.

'Thank you. I won't keep you from your work. Please carry on.' The girls went back to their writing but Jane could hear the adults' conversation. Miss Bilbrough's voice sounded strange, unlike anyone she'd heard before. Mr Quarrier introduced Reverend Millar to Miss Bilbrough and the two shook hands.

'Good morning, Reverend. What a pleasure to meet you. I must say, we in Canada are impressed with the ability of your children who have come to us already - you are doing a wonderful job.'

"We do our best, with the Lord's help, Miss Bilbrough. The girls are taught reading, writing and arithmetic by me, and practical skills by other staff. We are all grateful for the opportunity to improve their young lives.'

'Indeed. Just as we are - and all to our mutual advantage.'
All three nodded and smiled.

'This Junior class are aged up to eight years of age,' explained Mr Quarrier. 'The Seniors, who are aged from nine to twelve, are in their sewing class or training in the laundry just now. Please look around as you wish, then we will visit the other classes.'

Miss Bilbrough walked around the room, her long dress swishing. She looked over the girls' shoulders at their slates. Jane tried to write as neatly as possible, taking even more care than usual. She kept her eyes down in case she was asked something, but, after a few more minutes, the visitors moved on and the class returned to normal.

At dinner, Miss Bilbrough was standing with Miss Mathieson when the girls arrived. She watched closely as they moved to their places. Again she walked around the room, looking intensely at the young girls, speaking to some. The girls looked at each other and smiled, listening to the strange, loud drawl. But inside Jane felt very uncomfortable. She wanted this visit to end and Miss Bilbrough to go back to Canada, wherever that was. It seemed as if this visitor, with her piercing eyes and questions, would in some way change their lives. As usual when anxiety gnawed at her, her mind raced to John and when he would come for her.

That evening, the girls were led to the Hall they had cleaned. Around the table were seated many smartly-dressed strangers. Mr Quarrier and his wife were there, and a young woman was seated between them. 'That's Mr Quarrier's daughter,' whispered Kate. 'I've seen her in church.' The girls were arranged in rows at the end of the room. Tilly again stood between Jane and Kate for support, with Lizzie at her back. Jane thought how they had become like a little family. It was like having three more sisters nearer her age. They could never be like Ellen to her, but she was glad at least they were her friends and could be like sisters in the Home.

Reverend Millar stood before them and raised his hand for attention. In the corner, the pianist played a few chords. The guests around the table fell silent. At a signal from the minister, the girls began to sing and the room was filled with music. They sang several hymns, concluding with *Safe in the Arms of Jesus*. When they had finished, Reverend Millar bowed to the guests, who applauded warmly. He took his seat at the table as Miss Mathieson led the girls away, smiling and saying, 'Well done. That was splendid.'

Mr Quarrier rose. 'Good evening and welcome, dear friends. I am delighted to present our honoured guest, Miss Bilbrough of the Marchmont Receiving Home in Belleville, Ontario. After dinner, she will tell you of the work done there and of her plans for the future involving the children in our care. She and I have already discussed this, and I have no doubt, when you hear her speak, you will agree that there exist the most exciting opportunities which we would do well to grasp. For now, I will introduce you all briefly and we may talk at length later. On Miss Bilbrough's left is our esteemed Lord Provost of Glasgow, James Collins.' The Lord Provost said good evening and smiled at the other guests. 'Mr Galbraith some of you already know. He is responsible for the day to day running of this Home. On his left is Lord Alexander of Renfrew. Our remaining guests represent the business communities of Glasgow, Aberdeen, Montrose and Edinburgh.' Mr Quarrier continued to call out names and each person named nodded in turn. He then called to a housemaid positioned at the door, 'You may serve the food, please.'

The meal passed with quiet conversation around the table, while the guests ate their fill. When the last dishes had been removed, Mr Quarrier rose again.

'I'd now like to call upon Miss Bilbrough to address you.'

'Ladies and gentlemen, I thank Mr Quarrier and his staff for that hearty meal. It was much appreciated by me after so many days at sea. I am aware that you are very busy people and I thank you for coming to meet me this evening.' She then outlined the Canadian system for placing child migrants on farms, and said how she hoped that many girls from Scotland would now follow the boys who had already settled in Canada. 'Having visited the classrooms, kitchen and laundry today, I can see that these girls have learned skills which will make them very desirable workers. I am confident that when I visit the Cessnock Boys' Home tomorrow, I will find the same situation. Our farming communities desperately need workers; I know you have many here who will not find work or homes in Glasgow, or indeed in your other cities and towns, because of the thousands of people arriving from rural communities in Scotland and from Ireland.' She went on to talk about the benefits to children of growing up and working in the open air and living with families where they would have room to grow and thrive. She stressed that the children's education would continue and that they would attend church whenever possible. Around the room, people were nodding approvingly. 'They will be guaranteed work for a number of years and our inspectors visit host families to ensure that children are well cared for. Many children have asked me to bring messages to Mr Quarrier to say how grateful they are to have been sent to new homes and work. I will read you one, if I may.' She took a letter from her bag and read,

'Dear Mr and Mrs Quarrier,

I hope you are both well. I want to say how happy I am in this new land and to thank you for sending me here. I enjoy the work and when I go to church I pray that my new family are as happy as I am. They say they are. I also pray for my friends in Glasgow and hope that one day they will be able to come to Canada too.

Goodbye and God bless,

Davie Wilson

Clearly a happy boy, I'm sure you will agree. Mr Quarrier?'

'Thank you, Miss Bilbrough; that was very enlightening. Now, ladies and gentlemen, you know how hard we try to take as many children off our filthy streets as possible, but there are always many we have to leave. As quickly as we take them in, others take their places. They are at constant risk of disease and death. They are often victims of crime because they have no-one to protect them, but often they turn to crime themselves. This means that our prisons are also full of such young people. We as a community must strive to change this situation.'

He went on to discuss the progress of his Cottage Homes project in Bridge of Weir, but stressed that the problem remained of what happened to the orphans when they left his care. 'To combat this, we plan to send one hundred boys and girls to Canada with Miss Bilbrough in May. My wife, my daughter and I will accompany them on this trip so that we can see for ourselves the Canadian side of the migration scheme. This is timely, given the imminent expansion of the scheme in Scotland. All being well, we would like to send one hundred more young people on the next available sailing in December. None of this, of course, can happen without public support, particularly from the business community.' Guests looked at each other, sensing what would come next. 'I ask you to make a donation to allow our work to continue. You will be helping to train the future workforce as well as improving life in our great city. You will also have the gratitude of our Canadian colleagues. I implore you to help and I thank you again for coming this evening. We will now retire to the office where you are welcome to partake of a glass of fine port. If you have any questions about our work, Mr Galbraith, Miss Bilbrough and I will be happy to answer them.'

Some two hours later, Mr Quarrier closed the front door behind the last guest, breathing a sigh of relief. In the office, Mr Galbraith was writing down and adding up figures.

'I am hopeful from promises this evening that the next two trips to Canada can go ahead as planned.'

'Thank the Lord', said Mr Quarrier,' our faith in Him is always rewarded. You must be tired, Miss Bilbrough. Let us summon a carriage so that my family can now make you welcome. Tomorrow will be another busy day.'

'If today is anything to judge by, it will also be very worthwhile.'

12

John was bent over his machine, concentrating on stitching a shoe when Theresa appeared at his side. 'Mr Slowey wants you right away - in his office.' The other shoemakers looked up and raised their eyebrows. John hurried to the office, hoping he was not in trouble. Auld Slowey rarely sent for workers, though he often supervised their work.

'Sir? You sent for me?'

'Come in, John. Sit down.' He pointed to a seat facing him. John suddenly noticed Auld Slowey's daughter, Ann, seated at a desk. She was a pretty girl that he'd often seen in the workroom. She was writing in a huge ledger, but looked up and smiled at him. He nodded, conscious of his old, soiled clothes; he wiped the dust as best he could from his trousers before he sat down.

'John, I'm pleased to say I have prepared your papers; you are now officially a qualified Journeyman Shoemaker. I spoke to you before about staying on with me. Have you decided if you want to?'

'Sir, I'd like to stay on and become a Master Shoemaker like you. I know it's what my da would have wanted, may he rest in peace.'

'Good. I don't offer this to all my journeymen, John, but I like your work. You will now earn wages of eight shillings a week, as well as continuing your training. As I know your family circumstances, I'm prepared to offer you somewhere to stay. I've a room upstairs where three other journeymen in my employ bide. You could join them, I will take the rent of two shillings a week from your wages and you'll have the rest to keep. How does that sound?'

'I'd like that fine, sir.'

'In that case, you can begin immediately. Here are your Journeyman papers, signed by myself. Theresa will show you the room.' He rang a small brass bell on his desk.

'Take John to the journeymen's room, where he will be biding now. Good day, John.'

'Good day, Sir, and thank you. Good day, Miss.' Ann raised her head and smiled again.

John proudly clutched his papers to his chest and followed Theresa along the lobby where he had been sleeping. They mounted a staircase and Theresa opened the door facing them. Inside were four iron-framed beds and beside each one a small set of drawers. In the corner was a jawbox and on the back wall a fire; a table and four chairs stood in the middle of the room. Theresa pointed to a bed next to a small window.

'This'll be yours, John. You'll all share the jawbox and you can cook on the fire. Mr Slowey provides sheets but you must wash them yourselves. The others who stay here are Desmond, Harry and Jimmy. I'll leave you now.'

'Thanks, Theresa.'

John looked around the room. He carefully put his Journeyman papers in his drawer. His situation was at last improving and he wished he could tell his family: he knew they'd be happy for him, but he couldn't contact any of them. A horrible thought crept into his mind. *What if he was ill or even died? They wouldn't know.* But he mustn't think like that. He would work hard with Auld Slowey and try to save money, though he wouldn't be left with much after paying for his lodgings and buying food. He'd promised Jane he would find a place for them to live and he would, as soon as he was able. For now, she was at least being well cared for at the Orphan Home; he hoped she wasn't unhappy at all.

That night, he met his fellow lodgers; although he had seen them at work he didn't know them. Like him, they had no family homes. Desmond and Harry were young men - but Jimmy was older. He was stooped and looked weary.

'So you're to bide here too? Well it's better than the lobby or the street. We try to share our food to save money and time. We have potatoes for tonight and a few nights more. When you get paid you can put towards the next food we buy.'

'I will, Jimmy. I'm much obliged.'

'I see Auld Slowey has given you sheets', Desmond said. 'They won't keep you warm during the night when the fire is out. You'd do well to find a blanket or old coat.'

'I will - as soon as I get my wages.' John was embarrassed that he had no possessions and decided he would go to nearby Paddy's Market.

He knew that many Irish people went there looking for cheap second-hand clothes and household goods. He had gone with his own mother. *Don't pay the first price asked for. Remember to always give things a shake before you buy, John, and watch for fleas moving.* An old blanket or coat would be easy to find once he had money in his pocket.

'Here,' said Harry, handing John a ragged coat. 'Use this till you get something; I only use it if I go out and that's not often.'

'Thanks, Harry. Thank you all for your kindness.' In bed that night, he lay listening to the unfamiliar sounds of snoring and muttering in the room. He could smell sweat and the musty odour of dampness from Harry's coat but was glad of it to cover him; having a bed to sleep in made up for any inconvenience.

13

The May sun shone brightly. Like little sunflowers, the girls lifted their faces to its warmth. Jane played *Ring o' Roses* with Kate and Lizzie while Tilly looked on, clapping in time to their song. At the words "we all fall down", they dropped to the ground, laughing. Suddenly, a shadow fell across them and they looked up to see Dr Matthews looming over them. 'I need to see you, Tilly. Come with me. Kate, Mr Galbraith wants you in his office at once.' The bell rang to signal the end of break and Jane and Lizzie lined up for class, wondering what could be going on.

Tilly limped along beside Dr Matthews, trying to keep up with his long strides. He slowed down and took Tilly's hand as they climbed the stairs. 'I have good news for you this fine morning, Tilly. Your new boot has arrived. We're going to see how it fits.' In his surgery, Dr Matthews opened a large box and took out a boot that seemed enormous. 'Take off your old boot, Tilly, and I'll explain how this one works.' He held the large leather boot out and pointed to the sole, which was deeper than usual. 'This is to make up for the difference in the lengths of your legs. Once you have the boot on, you shouldn't have to limp. The sides are longer too, with built-in struts to help support your leg. Let's try it.'

Tilly sat while Dr Mathews put the boot on. He tightened straps around it. The sides felt hard against her leg. 'Stand up, Tilly. I'll hold your hand till you get your balance.' Tilly stood and felt the difference at once. She didn't lean sideways as she usually did. 'Now try to walk. It might take some getting used to.' Holding his hand tightly, Tilly stepped forward in the new boot, but almost fell with the weight of it. 'Take your time. It will feel strange at first. You should practise with the rails for a while.' He led Tilly to two rails fixed onto the floor. He adjusted the rails so that they were at the height of Tilly's hand. 'Just keep walking backwards and forwards till you can do it easily.' Tilly tried walking. When she lifted her 'good' foot, the pressure on her short leg was painful because of the struts in the sides of the boot. She felt the edge of the boot catch on her knee. When she lifted the new boot, it was so heavy that she gasped each time she tried to position it in front. She couldn't control it and it hit her other ankle as it passed. She felt tears coming and tried to hold them back. 'You must persevere, Tilly. If this doesn't work, there's really nothing else to be done. You've tried a crutch before and couldn't manage it.'

Tilly thought he sounded angry. She had tried using the crutch he had given her, but it was too difficult to use on the stairs, and she had fallen over in the yard a few times when the cobbles were slippery with rain. She preferred after a while to just limp. She was used to that, and to the mocking comments people made. Her stepfather had said she must be wicked to have a deformity like that. Dr Matthews had explained that her limp was there because she had been ill as a small child. 'I'll keep trying, Doctor. I'm sure it'll be alright.' He had been kind to her - she did not want to disappoint him. With great difficulty, Tilly walked back and forth along the rails.

Dr Matthews watched for a while, then said, 'I have to see some patients, Tilly. Keep going - but take a rest if you are very tired.' He left a chair at one end of the rails which Tilly sank into as soon as he had left the room. Wincing, she touched her leg where the top of the boot had rubbed against it. It felt so comfortable to just sit and ease the pain, but, after a few minutes, she started walking again, worried that the doctor might come back and think she wasn't trying. When the bell rang for dinner, Dr Matthews came back and helped her down to the dining hall. Seated beside Jane and Lizzie, she felt more comfortable and tried not to think about the pain and the worry that she would never get used to the new 'gift'. When her friends asked about her new boot and if it helped, she simply shrugged her shoulders. Just as they were wondering where Kate had got to, she arrived, looking pale and agitated.

'I'm going to Canada with Mr and Mrs Quarrier in two weeks, but when they come back I have to stay there with a family. Girls from the Senior class are going too, but they'll be in different families.'

'Do you want to go?' asked Jane.

'No, but Mr Galbraith said I have to. He said it's a wonderful chance to have a better life. I want to go to the new village with you.' Her lip quivered and her voice trembled. The others shook their heads, astounded that Kate would be going somewhere without them and not be coming back. Dinner was eaten in silence. They felt they should be happy for Kate, but, since they could not imagine Canada, she might as well be going to the moon.

That night, Jane couldn't sleep. She thought of Kate and tried to imagine the Home without her. Kate had helped her since she arrived and now she seemed like a sister. *How many more people would she lose from her life?* She thought of Da and Ma and her brothers and sister. *How far away her life with them seemed now.*

Next morning, she felt tired and sad. She, Kate, Tilly and Lizzie sat together, hardly speaking. At breakfast, Miss Mathieson called the names of the girls going to Canada and told them to report to the Hall after breakfast where preparations were being made for their departure. Kate left her porridge, too anxious to eat. 'What if I don't like Canada? What if the family don't like me?' The others glanced at each other, not knowing how to comfort her. Lizzie suggested that if that happened, she should write to Mr Quarrier to see if she could be sent back. Kate nodded and set off for the Hall.

Mr Galbraith stood at the door of the Hall and as each girl arrived, he ticked a list. When all twenty were gathered, he took them into the Hall. Against the wall were twenty bundles of clothes and beside each a wooden trunk; Miss Mathieson stood at a table covered with boots. Mr Galbraith said, 'You girls are very fortunate. Mr Quarrier has provided an extra set of clothing and a cape for each of you to take to Canada. You will also receive a pair of boots, which Miss Mathieson will help you with. Take a bigger size than you are wearing so that they will last you longer. Trunks have been made for you by our boys in Cessnock and each one has a name on it - Miss Mathieson will help you find your own. When you leave for Canada, you may take one small personal belonging with you, but that is all; the weight of baggage on the ship is limited. I hope you all appreciate the wonderful opportunity you are being given and Thank God for it in your prayers.'

He left and Miss Mathieson walked alongside the bundles on the floor, calling out names. 'You must check that your clothes will fit, then pack them into your trunk. Come to the table for a pair of boots and these will also go in the trunk. If you have a personal belonging with you, put that in the trunk too; if not, bring it later today!' Kate checked all her clothes and chose her boots. She tried to tell herself how happy she should be to have all these clothes and to be going to a new life, but she could not imagine the future. Hot tears fell on her new clothes as she packed them. As soon as she could, she fled to the yard where Jane, Lizzie and Tilly were waiting to hear what had happened. When she saw them she could not speak for crying. Jane couldn't think of anything to say, but just held her hand softly instead. Kate wiped her face with her tunic and told them about her trunk of clothes. 'We can also take something of our own, but I haven't got anything.' When the bell rang, they went forlornly to sewing class. Jane suggested to the sewing teacher that they make a handkerchief for Kate to take to Canada.

'We could embroider her name on it too.'

'Good idea, Jane. I'm sure I can find a nice remnant for that.' The teacher then brought a square of cotton, stitched the edges and suggested they each stitch a letter of Kate's name. 'You do two, Jane, since you thought of it.' By the end of the class, the handkerchief was finished. Kate folded it neatly and ran to put it in her trunk, thinking again how much she would miss her friends.

14

John walked along by Glasgow Green with Desmond and Harry. In one arm he carried the clothes bought at Paddy's Market. In his pocket, he felt for the coins left from his wages and gripped them tightly. They were precious, but he was about to spend some in the newly-opened Greenhead Public Baths that Desmond and Harry had told him about. 'Anyone can go, and for a few pennies you can have a warm bath.' They'd also told him about a 'steamie' there, where clothes could be washed in giant tubs and hung to dry near stoves which heated the water. He could hardly believe it. *How Ma and Da would have loved it.* When they reached Greenhead Street, there were two queues formed outside the big new building, men in one and women in the other. It was over an hour before they got inside. At a window in a small cubicle stood a man who took their money and gave them tickets for baths and a piece of red soap each.

'We want to use the steamie too, but we'll share a tub for our clothes,' said Desmond.

'That'll be another thruppence ha'penny. Make sure you leave everything clean and tidy for the next person. The warden'll be checking on you.' Another ticket and more soap were handed over. When everything had been paid for, John still had some coins left. He'd be able to pay for his food at Auld Slowey's too. There would be little left after that, but he felt that life was getting better. They walked along a tiled corridor which smelled of strong soap, towards a room with a sign saying 'Men's Bathroom' above the door. Inside, John's eyes began stinging with the smell of soap and the steam. The warden, a tall man with a red, sweaty face pointed along a room lined with cubicles - small curtained-off areas, each with a bath. 'You've twenty minutes in the bath. Half fill it. When you've finished, rinse the bath with disinfectant from the jug on the floor. Don't leave anything behind, especially diseases. We're trying to get rid of those.' He laughed loudly and directed each of them to a cubicle, handing out towels.

Inside, John closed the curtain and, while the hot water poured into the bath, he undressed. His clothes were dirty and grimy; some of them seemed like a collection of threads instead of clothes. He piled them on the floor, wrinkling his nose at the smell. He laid his new clothes on a stool. When the bath was half full, he carefully climbed in. The warmth was wonderful and he scrubbed himself with soap. He leaned back and washed his hair. The water grew cloudy, then a scum appeared on top. He pushed it away from his body and stood up quickly. He stepped out and dried himself, letting the water away to miraculously gurgle down invisible pipes. With clean clothes on, he felt like a different person. He remembered to clean the bath with disinfectant, before going out into the corridor to meet Desmond and Harry. They laughed at each other's bright red faces.

Next they ventured into the laundry. Hot steam rose in clouds from tubs around the room. Theirs was in a stall in the far corner. As they were led towards it, women called out and laughed at the sight of them, the only men in the room apart from the man in charge, who said, 'Dinnae worry about them, lads. They think they rule the roost here, but I'm the boss.' He showed them how to fill the tub. 'When you put in your dirty clothes, use this stick to birl them roon' so the soap gets through them a'. Let the dirty water awa' by pullin' this chain. Then rinse the clothes in fresh water and wring them out in the big sink. Hang them to dry on this since you dinnae hae much.' He pulled out a large wooden frame from against the wall. 'If ye cannae manage, I'm sure some of these fine lassies'll help you.' With a loud guffaw, he left them.

Gingerly, they put their clothes in the tub. They took turns swirling the clothes around, turning the water grey and grimy. They let it away, then rinsed the clothes till there was no soap left. Each took his own clothes and tried to wring the water out of them till they stopped dripping. John felt the water run up his arms, wetting his clean clothes. Too late, he noticed how all the women had rolled up their sleeves or had bare arms. He marvelled at how they were able to wring huge sheets as well as clothes - obviously they'd had lots of practice. The men hung up their clothes, happy to have managed their first 'washing'. As they passed through the steamie, one woman called out, 'Wid ye luk at thae glaikit lumps. Three ae thum needit tae dae a wee wash. They cannae huv a wummin tae dae it fur thum. Is that no' right, boys?'

Women howled with laughter as John and the others hurried by, their faces scarlet.

'That was awful, but at least we know what to do. Maybe we could take turns at coming in future.'

'Aye, definitely, John', said Desmond, 'and we could bring the bed-sheets too.' As they walked past the Green, they saw women from the steamie carrying huge bundles of washing wrapped in sheets slung over their shoulders. They took their 'bagwash' and hung it on washing lines on the Green, where it blew in the warm May breeze.

Back at Schipka Pass, he put his clothes away, proud that he now had two sets. Full of optimism, he decided to go back for a walk in the sunshine. When he passed through the lobby, Ann Slowey came out of her office.

'Good afternoon, John. How are you?'

'I'm very well, thanks, Miss.' He could see Ann glancing at his clothes and was glad they were clean and that he'd had a bath. She always looked clean and tidy as well as pretty.

'Going out?'

'It's nice weather. I thought I'd walk through the Green for a while, Miss.'

'What a lovely idea.' She hesitated. 'Could I come? I don't like walking in the streets myself but I'd love a walk beside the river. I seldom have time.' John blushed. He'd often wished he could spend time with Ann, but because she was his master's daughter he would never have asked her out.

'Of course, Miss. I'd like that fine.'

'Call me Ann, John.'

'Thank you, Miss. I mean Ann.' As they walked along, Ann told him how pleased her father was with his work, and, strangely, John felt comfortable enough to talk about his own family. He talked about Jane and how he desperately wanted to take her out of the orphanage, but needed a home to take her to.

'I don't have brothers or sisters and my mother died a long time ago, but I wouldn't like to be separated from my father. I can understand why you're so sad. But you're a good man, John, and a hard worker. I'm sure you'll do it one day.' As they walked along the banks of the Clyde, talking about their lives, John's heart felt lighter than it had for a long time. Ann was such a lovely companion. He couldn't believe his luck when she said, 'I must go home now, John, but I hope we can do this again.' Suddenly his whole future seemed brighter.

15

'I wonder how Kate is,' said Lizzie. Jane's face clouded. She had been wondering the same thing ever since Kate had left. Mr Quarrier had returned from the trip to Canada, full of praise for 'the work being done over there for our fortunate young people'. He had announced at a church service that all the children who had sailed with him were now with new families and had a bright new future ahead of them. He had again asked the parishioners to donate funds so that more children could be rescued from 'the evils of poverty and disease in our midst'. He mentioned the building of the new village which was almost ready. Still Jane had not heard from John or Ellen. Lizzie and Tilly consoled her with their friendship, but she longed for her own family.

Almost as soon as the twenty girls chosen had left for Canada, twenty more girls arrived at the Orphan Home. Suddenly, Jane found herself helping them, as she now knew the daily routines and where everything was. It seemed as if she had been there for years - not just a few short months. One girl, Mary, now sat with Jane and the others. When she'd arrived at the Home, Mary had had to have her hair cut off because she had lice. It made her look strange and even thinner than she was. Jane felt sorry for Mary when some of the others laughed at her, and she had brought her to sit beside her and Tilly and Lizzie.

'Who is Kate? Is she sick?' asked Mary.

'No, she's our friend but she got sent to Canada,' replied Jane.

'What's that?'

'It's a country far away. We don't really know about it. Kate went to live there with a new family.'

'We don't think we'll ever see her again,' said Lizzie. 'I hope her new family aren't like my stepfather. He was horrible – not like a real da.'

'I had a stepfather too. He was nice, but when my ma died he had to go far away to work so he brought me here,' said Mary.

'Why did he not take you with him if he was nice?'

'He said he couldn't; there was no room for me where he was going. If he can, he'll come back for me - that's what he said.' Jane thought about John's promise to come back for her. She didn't doubt him. At least he was in Glasgow. She felt comforted knowing he wasn't far away like Mary's stepfather. And Mr Galbraith had written to him, so she knew she shouldn't worry. What did it say in the Bible? 'Seek and ye shall find me'? If people could find God, surely John could find her. Still, she was worried. As the months went on, the faces of her family seemed to be fading in her memory. She needed to see them again soon.

16

Duke Street was coming to life in the early morning as a weak sun came up. Carriages rumbled along the cobblestones, taking merchants to offices where fortunes were being made from foreign trade; people pushed handcarts of goods to markets in the city; horses pulled wagons of coal. Coalmen urged them on with their heavy loads, to be delivered to grand houses or factories in time for fires to be lit or boilers to be stoked; the daily life of the city continued. Hearing the noise, people sleeping in doorways and closes woke up and emerged to begin their daily tramp, begging for food to stay alive. In front of the huge gates of Duke Street Prison, a wagon stopped. The door was opened by the burly gatekeeper and the driver asked,

'Any deid this mornin', Angus?'

'A few, Rab, but you should manage them all in one run.' He took a huge bundle of keys from his pocket and opened the gate. Rab grasped his horse's reins and led it into the yard. Behind the high prison walls, where the morning sun could not yet reach, the cobblestones were slippery with damp and moss. Another set of gates creaked open and two men pushed wooden carts towards the wagon. The smell was sickening; though he had been collecting dead bodies all his working life, Rab pulled the large scarf he was wearing round his neck up over his mouth. The two men loaded the corpses onto the wagon. 'None from Consumption this morning. All dead from natural causes.' One glance at the bodies of two women, three men and two small boys and it was obvious that death in prison wasn't natural at all, but then hunger and poverty didn't count as causes of death. Rab shook his head, climbed aboard his wagon and headed to the city mortuary.

Inside the prison, in a stone room with a small window high up on the wall, Ellen Anderson stirred from her restless sleep. She had been dreaming of her children; of holding them and singing them to sleep. Waking each morning to realise she was still in her prison cell broke her heart. She thought of Henry, and wondered if he was managing to keep her children from the Poorhouse. Hopefully, Jane would help look after them but she was just a child herself. Ellen looked around the cell at the other women; some huddled together for warmth, grey faces matching their prison tunics. From nearby came the sound of the guard's keys, striking the bars of cells to wake the sleeping women. Soon he reached theirs. 'Up, you lazy lot - thae piles of rocks outside won't break themselves. And mind you eat your breakfast without complaining; you'll need all the strength you can muster. Hurry along now!' As he opened their cell door and moved to the next one, the women groaned. Maggie, the oldest prisoner in the cell, muttered, 'More bloomin' rocks. I see them in ma sleep; when ah'm no' sleepin' ah've got ma achin' muscles to remind me o' them.'

Ellen's muscles ached too, though she was younger and fitter than Maggie. Month after month of breaking huge rocks into small stones with hammers and loading them into barrows had also given her calloused hands. She had bruises on her back and legs from being prodded with sticks when the guards thought she should be working harder. She hated them. At first, she'd fought back, shouting and pushing them away, but each time she had been taken to the Prison Governor and more weeks were added to her sentence. Now she simply kept going by imagining herself outside the prison walls. She was determined she would find a job when she was released so that she wouldn't have to beg and steal to feed her family.

She had been doing laundry for a rich merchant's family and taking it to hang on Glasgow Green to dry. It was hard work, but she was happy to be earning money and had done it for several months. One day, when the washing was almost dry, it began to rain and Ellen quickly pulled the clothes from the line, wrapping them in a sheet which she threw across her shoulder, and headed back to the merchant's house to deliver them. She handed them over to the maid for ironing, and gratefully took the few pence she had earned.

'Will there be more washing tomorrow?' she asked.

'Aye, come by aboot 10 when the rooms hae been cleaned. There'll be plenty then,' Next morning when Ellen arrived at the back door of the grand house, the maid looked flustered and said, 'The mistress wants tae speak tae ye. Ye'd best come in.' Ellen hoped they had more work for her, perhaps in the house itself instead of the wash-house in the back yard. She stood in the hallway and waited hopefully. From upstairs came the sound of quick footsteps, then the shrill sound of the merchant's wife, calling out as she came to face Ellen.

'So this is the thief? Shameless enough to come back here and expect to be trusted again. Where is my dress? Is it in your house or have you sold it already?'

'What dress? I don't know what you mean.'

'My green Merino wool dress that I was particularly fond of. You took it yesterday and didn't bring it back.' Ellen thought back to the previous day. She remembered washing the dress and hanging it up - but didn't remember taking it down with the other clothes.

'I must have left it on the line when the rain came on. I'll go and look, Ma'am.'

'You'd best hope it is there, though I have my doubts. If you have stolen it, you have this one chance to return it to me.' With sinking heart, Ellen ran to the Green where other women were hanging out clothes. She searched and searched and asked if anyone had seen the dress. No-one had. Frantic in case she lost the job, she returned to the merchant's wife and offered to do work for no pay to make up for the loss. Instead the woman had her arrested.

She could still remember the shame of being taken before the Magistrate accused of theft. 'Well, what have you to say for yourself?' She gave her honest account of what had happened but her story had not been believed. 'This court has no reason to disbelieve your employer and no reason to trust what you say. Some time in Duke Street with the opportunity to reflect on your wickedness will hopefully help you change your ways.' Ellen had spent those first ten days in Duke Street prison, determined that they would be her last.

Back outside, with no work or prospects, she had begged on the streets. She couldn't ask her mother for help as she was too ill. Henry suffered from bronchial disease and couldn't work, as the slightest effort exhausted him. Jane begged with her on the streets. When her mother died, Ellen had taken Jane in - another mouth to feed, but she had no choice. Eventually Ellen felt compelled to steal in order to feed her family. Each time she was caught, she went to prison for longer. She was hardened to it, but she knew that eventually disease and hardship would defeat her. She didn't want to die a criminal. She wanted to go home to her family, to care for them; the sooner this prison sentence was over, the sooner she could do that. Sorrowfully, she followed her cell-mates to start another dreadful day.

17

September arrived and Jane had still not heard from John. She was sad but was sure he'd be trying to find a place for them to live. In the meantime, she kept working hard at her reading, writing, sewing and washing so that she would be able to help look after their home when they were finally together.

One Friday evening, there was an assembly in the large upstairs hall. As usual, Jane went with her friends.

'I hope this is worth getting up these stairs for', sighed Tilly.

'I heard Miss Mathieson say Mr Quarrier's here, so maybe it'll be him.' Sure enough, when they entered the hall, they saw Mr Quarrier standing with Mr Galbraith at the front of the room.

'Mr Quarrier has a very important announcement for you. Pay close attention.'

'Good evening. It pleases me greatly to see you all looking so well in our care. I'm sure you all know how lucky you are to be here. Now your lives are about to improve even more. I am delighted to say that some of you will be the first children to go to cottages in our new village. As more cottages are completed, more of you will follow. In each cottage, there will be a House Mother and Father to care for you. You will be housed with other girls from here and some boys from our Cessnock Home. There will be a schoolroom and workrooms so that you can continue your training for later life. There will be garden areas to walk and play in and lovely fresh air to keep you healthy. In the last few days, many important guests have visited our village and all are agreed that it will be a wonderful opportunity for you all to go there. I'm able to tell you that the following girls will leave tomorrow.' He then began to call out names. Tilly, Mary and Lizzie's were all called out with others. Tilly clutched Jane's arm. 'I hope you're going too, Jane.' Jane hoped she wasn't, but at last her name was called. She felt as if a little bird was flapping its wings in her chest, trying to get out. *What about John and Ellen?* She would be further away from them now, but she reminded herself that at least Mr Galbraith had told John where she would be going. She knew they would seek her out when the time was right. Jane didn't sleep well. She dreamed of her parents. In the dream, she climbed in beside her mother in the big recess bed, hearing her whisper 'Coorie in, now,' but when Jane tried to cuddle her there was no-one there. 'Jane, Jane, what is it?' When she opened her eyes, Mary was beside her. 'Don't cry, Jane. You were shouting and woke me up.' Just then, Mrs Mathieson came into the dormitory. 'Come along, girls. We have a busy day ahead of us. Quickly – time to get up.' Jane got out of bed, rubbing tears from her eyes with her nightshirt. 'Just think', said Mary, 'This will be the last time we get washed in here. Tomorrow we'll be in our new home.' Mary's newly-grown brown curls bobbed as she spoke and clapped her hands. Jane wished she felt excited. All she could think about was whether she would ever be back with her family again.

At Grace, Miss Mathieson said a special prayer for those girls leaving them that morning, that the good Lord would bring them health and happiness in their new home. She then urged the 'travellers' to eat well in preparation for their journey. 'I am travelling with you and we should reach Bridge of Weir in time for dinner - there will be nothing more to eat before then. When breakfast is over, put on your capes and bonnets and wait in the yard for me.' Jane tried to eat, but again she felt imaginary wings flapping in her chest, and her stomach churned wildly. She managed a little porridge, milk and a bit of bread but could not finish her food.

Outside in the yard, Tilly, Lizzie and Mary stood around her and Tilly held her hand but Jane couldn't stop herself crying. Just as she felt she must tell Mr Galbraith that she wanted to stay, Miss Mathieson swept across the yard towards her.

'Dry your eyes at once, Jane. Why are you crying? In a few hours, you will be in a new home in beautiful surroundings. I hope you are not ungrateful after everything that has been done for you. Believe me, there are many girls who would like to be in your position. Do you want to be back on the streets?'

'No, Miss Mathieson.' Jane breathed deeply and dried her tears with her cape.

'Good. Now, line up with the others in twos.' Jane took Tilly's hand and told herself that Tilly needed her. *Who would help her if she didn't go?* This calmed her a little. As Miss Mathieson led the line of girls across the yard, other girls waved them goodbye. They passed through the hallway on their way out and Jane thought back to the first night she had arrived: how long ago it seemed now. Mr Galbraith came out of his office to see them off. 'Goodbye and good luck, girls. Remember the skills and good manners you have been taught here and put them to good use. Remember always to thank God for your good fortune and keep Mr Quarrier in your prayers.'

Outside the Home, four horse carriages were lined up. The girls were helped up steps into the coaches to sit on wooden benches inside. Miss Mathieson sat beside Jane. When everyone was on board, the carriage doors were closed. They moved over the cobbles and the girls were bumped up and down on the wooden seats. Jane felt sure she would have fallen off if Miss Mathieson had not been at her side. Tilly looked pale and was biting her lip as her heavy boot swung back and forth at each bump and Jane felt ashamed at having cried earlier when she realised how difficult this must be for her friend.

Out of the window, she glimpsed a corner of Glasgow Green, then the River Clyde before lots of unfamiliar buildings in the city. From where she sat she couldn't see the people they were passing, but could hear the everyday noises of the city that she had missed in the Home: voices of stall holders shouting out their wares of seafood, newspapers and clothes; bells ringing on carriages; children shouting and dogs barking. The carriages stopped and the coachman opened their door. 'St. Enoch's Station, Miss.' He helped Miss Mathieson back down the steps, then each of the girls. They were in front of a huge building which Jane had never seen before. Hundreds of people were coming and going through its iron gates; well-dressed ladies and men, with boys pushing carts of luggage behind them. Beside the gates, ragged women with children begged from passers-by; Jane thought of Ellen and wondered if she was still in Duke Street Prison or begging somewhere on the streets like these women. 'Line up in twos again, girls, and stay near me.' Miss Mathieson led them into the station towards a long, low building where men sat behind open windows with iron grilles. Miss Mathieson approached.

'Tickets for 20 children to Bridge of Weir, please, and one return ticket for me.'

'You'll want the Greenock train which leaves in fifteen minutes from Platform 5 at the end of the concourse.' He pointed to an iron gate with a huge number 5 on top and handed over the tickets in return for the money. Jane held tightly onto Tilly's hand and behind them walked Lizzie and Mary, ready to catch Tilly if she stumbled. They followed Miss Mathieson across the busy station.

'Anybody been on a train before?' asked Mary.

'Never' said Lizzie. The others shook their heads, eyes wide. They could see trains lined up at several platforms, smoke gushing noisily from their chimneys. To Jane, they seemed like huge, black monsters breathing smoke and steam. A guard in uniform and cap called, 'Tickets, please,' and when Miss Mathieson handed them over, he counted them, then counted the girls. He handed the tickets back, saying, 'They may be checked again aboard the train, so keep them safe - and don't let the children wander about inside the train.'

Inside, a long corridor ran along the train and off this corridor were sliding doors into compartments, each one with a long leather bench on each side and racks above them. The girls were put in two compartments which were side by side. Jane, Mary, Tilly and Lizzie were in one with six other girls. 'Listen carefully, girls. You must stay in your seats throughout the journey but the passing landscape will be interesting and watching it will pass the time. If I am not with you, I will be next door or in the corridor. You may speak quietly to each other but to no-one else.' Just then, a noisy group of boys, all dressed alike in jackets, caps and breeches, were led along the platform and into their carriage. A man with them called out,

'Good morning, Miss Mathieson. Which compartments are your group in?'

'These two beside me, Mr Martin. The next two are vacant.'

'Excellent. Then we will use them and you and I can share the supervision.' The two shook hands and the boys were put in compartments with the same instructions as the girls. 'They must be the boys from the other Home that Mr Quarrier was speakin' aboot,' said Lizzie; Mary tried to answer but the noise of a loud horn and the hissing of steam drowned out what she said. The girls held their ears in mock terror. They heard the sound of carriage doors slamming shut, Miss

Mathieson slid their compartment door closed and the train began to move. They could feel the movement of the train along the tracks underneath them and steam flew past their windows like clouds. Railway sheds and signal boxes went by as the steam cleared, then all they could see was sky.

'I think we must be flying - where's the ground? The girl nearest the window stood up to look out.

'We're on a bridge, crossin' ower water.' As other girls clustered around to see out, one called in panic,

'Dinnae a' look oot thegither. The train might fa' ower into the water.' They laughed hysterically and ran back to their seats. Hearing the commotion, Miss Mathieson slid open the door and looked in. 'We are crossing the River Clyde. You are perfectly safe but I want you to stay in your seats as we will be stopping at other stations and I don't want anyone else joining us.'

Once over the bridge, the train turned slightly and settled to a steady speed, passing houses and shops on one side and going alongside the Clyde on the other. 'Look at all the boats' cried Mary, 'We're going faster than them.' An assortment of ships and smaller boats went in both directions, trailing smoke as they went. The train veered again and the river disappeared. 'There's some houses. Maybe we're nearly there.' Tilly pointed out of the window, but the houses were already disappearing into the distance. The train began to slow down and soon chugged into one station after another. At each one, people got off and on, looking as if this was perfectly normal - Jane could not believe her eyes. When Miss Mathieson next put her head round the door, Lizzie asked,

'Are we getting off now?'

'No, we're just at Paisley, but we'll be there soon.'

The landscape changed again. All around were fields, some with cows or sheep in them. The few houses to be seen were low buildings with tiny windows, very different from Glasgow tenements. In the distance, the river came back into view. As Jane gazed across the fields, rain began pattering against the window, blurring and changing the shape of everything outside. It made Jane think of her dream and how her memory of Ma and Da was now blurred and the shape of her life had changed. Like the view from the window, it didn't seem real.

18

'Almost there, girls. Come and line up in the corridor.' The girls followed Miss Mathieson into the corridor, where they stood swaying to the motion of the train. Further along, they could see the boys who had got on the train in Glasgow. Outside the window, rain-swept fields rolled by as the train began to slow down, hissing and hooting. At last it stopped and the girls tumbled into each other, laughing and grabbing at the window frames to stay upright. When the doors were opened, they were glad to climb down onto a platform which didn't move beneath their feet. A gust of wind blew through the station, clutching at caps and bonnets. 'Stand back from the track, girls and boys. Into the waiting-room out of the wind and rain.' Mr Martin opened the door of a wooden building and they filed in. By the time they were all inside, the train had gone. The boys and girls looked curiously at each other, but no-one spoke. Moments later, the door opened and a large red-faced man came in.

'Good morning, all. You must be Miss Mathieson and Mr Martin. I'm Mr Alexander. Welcome to Bridge of Weir. The carriages are outside waiting.' The adults shook hands. 'It's a pity it's raining as I only have open carriages available today, but the journey is a short one. Follow me, please.' Four horse-drawn carts stood ready, the horses snuffling and shaking their heads in the rain. In each cart were two wooden benches and a box stood at the side of each cart for stepping on. 'Climb on quickly, children; girls in the front two and boys in the others.' The boys and girls climbed in as quickly as they could. Jane struggled to help Tilly onto the box, but Mr Alexander lifted her into the air and onto a seat in one motion. Tilly laughed delightedly. When everyone was settled, the drivers flapped their reins and the horses moved off. They turned onto a cobbled road and the girls were bounced around on the benches, with the wind and rain in their faces. 'This is like being at the Fair on Glasgow Green' cried Mary. Exhilarated, they oohed and aahed each time they were bounced in the air. Tilly tried to say something to Jane, but her words were drowned out by the noise of the carriage wheels and the howling, biting wind. Jane raised her eyes and shook her head. A few houses came into view. Jane hoped this was their destination, but then they passed these houses and turned into a lane with trees and bushes on each side, and fields beyond them. At each bend, Jane expected the village to appear but it didn't; they seemed to have come such a long way.

At last the carriage in front turned through two large gates. Ahead they could see several large buildings; some stone-built houses and a larger building. Beyond these, fields stretched into the distance and animals in them looked like tiny specks. The girls' carriages stopped in front of one house, the boys' carriages at another. The door of the large house opened and a man and woman appeared in the doorway. The woman wore a grey dress with an apron over it and a white cap; grey curls escaped from the lacy edge of the cap. She held the door open. 'Come away in, girls. What a day for your arrival.' The girls ran inside, rain dripping from their clothes and boots, and found themselves in a large hallway with a grand staircase. Several large wooden doors led into rooms around the hallway. 'Here is the cloakroom. It is organised for you, so find the peg with your name above it and hang up your capes and bonnets, leave your boots beneath them, then follow me. You are going to have a bath and change of clothes. We don't want anyone getting a chill. I am your House Mother, Mrs Brown, and my husband is your House Father - we'll get to know each other later.' In a large bathroom on the ground floor, two women were filling several baths with warm water. 'When it's your turn, leave your clothes in this basket for washing. You will be given new, clean clothes once you are washed. Towels are on the shelf there. While you are waiting for a bath, stand in the corridor. When you have bathed and changed, you can wait in the dining-room across the hallway. Don't wander anywhere else. You will see the rest of the house after dinner.' Mrs Brown left them to their bathing.

Warmed from the hot bath and fresh clothes, Jane joined the others in the dining-room, a lot smaller than the one at the Home. Lizzie was getting restless.

'Come and see what else there is, Jane?'

'We're supposed to stay here.'

'We can say we need to go to the lavatory. Come on.' Hearing voices, they tiptoed in their stocking feet along the corridor towards the sitting-room. The large wooden door was ajar and the girls kept close to the wall. Through the space between the door and its surround they could see Miss Mathieson in a large armchair beside a roaring coal fire. Her cape and bonnet were being dried on a frame near the fire. They heard the voice of Mrs Brown.

'Will you join us for dinner, Miss Mathieson? It will be ready within the hour.'

'I won't, thanks, as I'm going back to Glasgow on the next train. A driver is coming back for me. However, I'm enjoying this cup of tea; you're very kind. This is a lovely house - Mr Quarrier must be very proud.' They could hear the rattle of china cups.

'It's a very nice house. We're looking forward to working here. I'm sure the village will be a great success. It will be good for the children to get out of the city.'

'It will be. You probably know already about the plans to send some of them to the Canadian countryside.' Lizzie shook Jane's arm and they looked at each other open-mouthed.

'We were told about that. Do you know when it will be?

'Mr Galbraith will contact you in due course, I'm sure.' A bell sounded and they heard Mr Brown say,

'Your carriage is here, Miss Mathieson, and the rain has gone off so your return trip should be more comfortable.'

'I thank you both and wish you well in your new employment. I will see you next time I come.'

The girls hurried back along the corridor, sliding on the new linoleum. From the dining-room window, they saw Miss Mathieson leave the house and climb into the carriage without a backward glance.

'I wonder why she didn't say goodbye', said Lizzie.

'Maybe she's forgotten us already', said Jane, turning sadly away. She wondered how many more people would come in and out of her life.

19

'John, John, can you help me?' John was in the workshop when Ann ran in.

'My father's ill. Can you stay with him till I bring the doctor? His breathing's very bad.'

'Certainly, Ann.' He followed her to the top floor of the building. Auld Slowey lay in bed in a small room. His breath was rasping and John was shocked to see how grey his skin was.

'John will stay with you till I bring the doctor, Father. I'll be as quick as I can.' She took a cape from behind the door and left, running. Auld Slowey's eyelids fluttered and he tried to raise an arm, but couldn't speak. He had not been in the workshop for a week or two and Ann had said he wasn't well, but he looked really ill now. He reminded John of his father before he died. A spasm of coughing shook his thin body and specks of blood came from his mouth. John took a towel from the rail on the kitchen range and wet it under the water spigot. Gently, he wiped, wetting his master's dry lips and clearing the blood from his cheek.

'Ann...'

'Try not to speak, Mr Slowey. Save your breath. She's gone for the doctor and they'll be here soon.' The old man grew more agitated.

'Mind Ann... for me.' John thought he heard him whisper 'dying', then he sank back onto his pillow.

'Don't worry, Mr Slowey. I'll look after her.'
John and Ann had become great friends over the previous months. He knew how worried she was about her father, having no mother, brothers or sisters to turn to. More and more, she relied on John in the workshop when her father couldn't come in. Auld Slowey had taught John well and he enjoyed the extra responsibility; it would be good experience for him if he had to find another job.

John rearranged the covers around the old man. His rasping breath grew louder, his hands flapped and John held them to settle him. They felt clammy and trembled. He was terribly weak. At last, John heard Ann's quick footsteps on the stairs. She came in, followed by a doctor carrying a large leather bag. John stood up to let him approach the bed.

'John, thanks for staying with Father. Can you see to things in the workshop for now?'

'Of course.' Glad to be away from the sick-bed, John quickly left.

The doctor bent over Auld Slowey, listening to his breathing and feeling his forehead.

'I fear he's much worse than when I saw him a few days ago, Miss Slowey. The Consumption has progressed rapidly. I'll try to have him taken into Belvidere Hospital, but they're very short of beds. In the meantime, keep him cool and comfortable. Try to open a window to let air in. He is shivering, I know, but that is caused by fever. I'll contact the hospital and come back this evening.'

'Thank you, Doctor.' Ann showed him out, opened a window then returned to sit by her father. She hadn't slept much during the night. She felt exhausted and was fighting back tears. She wished John Anderson was with her, but she needed him to take charge in the workshop. Maybe once her father had gone to hospital they could spend some time together and she could thank him for his support. Another spasm of coughing shook her father's body. More blood appeared from his mouth and Ann quickly wiped it away. His eyes opened and he grasped her hand.

'John…good man for you.'

'I know, Father, but try to rest now. John will help me in the workshop till you're better.' Her father nodded and his eyes closed again. He sank back, exhausted.

At the end of the working day, John went back upstairs to the Sloweys' flat. Ann had not moved from her father and she looked pale and tired. The old man seemed in a deep sleep.

'I can stay with him till you go and eat and rest, Ann. You'll make yourself ill too if you don't.'

'I don't think I can eat, but a cup of tea would be very welcome. I'm obliged to you, John, for helping me - I'm so afraid for my father.'

'I know, Ann, and I'm happy to help.'

'I'll be in the kitchen. Call me if you think he's worse.'

'I will, I promise.' Again John sat with Auld Slowey and tried to make him comfortable, but the sick man no longer tried to speak or open his eyes; his breathing became harsher and louder with every passing moment. Soon, Ann returned. They could hear footsteps on the stairs, and Theresa appeared with the doctor. She left as quickly as she could, covering her mouth with her apron and avoiding the sight of the old man.

'I'm sorry, Miss Slowey - but Belvidere can't take him. They have no beds available. I could send him to the hospital wing at Barnhill, but to be frank, I think the journey would finish him off. He's more comfortable here. I'm afraid the Consumption cannot be cured - you must prepare yourself for the worst.' Ann's lip trembled and John reached for her hand. He wished he could bring her more solace but could only think that the sooner her father's suffering was over the better.

When the doctor left, John went to his room to eat, promising to come back as soon as he could. When he told his fellow lodgers how ill Auld Slowey was, they were immediately worried.

'Did the doctor say how long he'll live?' said Harry.

'No, but not long, I think' Jimmy shook his head.

'So we'll all be looking for jobs soon? The workshop cannot be run by thon young lassie of his. Maybe with a brother it would have been possible, but not on her own.' John quickly defended Ann.

'She's helped her father run things for years and knows all about the work and the trade.'

'But who's going to take orders from a lass? No, we'll all be out on the street soon, you mark my words.' John's heart felt heavy. Just when he thought things were going well for him, it seemed another crisis was looming. They ate in gloomy silence.

When John returned to the Sloweys' flat, the door was lying open. He could hear Auld Slowey's breath rattling in his chest. Ann was still beside him, holding his hand.

'Will I stay with you, Ann? What can I do?'

'Just sit with me, John. I keep thinking his breathing has stopped, but then that awful rattling noise starts up again. He hasn't opened his eyes for hours. I don't think he can last much longer.' Just then, her father moaned and tried to lift his arm. Ann held his hand.

'I'm here, Father.' His lips moved but no words came. His breathing stopped and this time did not start again. His hand grew heavy in Ann's, and she laid his arm across his thin body.

'He's gone, hasn't he, John?'

'I'm afraid so, my dear.' Ann's tears came then and John held her close till she was calm again. 'The doctor will need to come in again to check him and write a death certificate. Maybe Theresa could fetch him for you.'

Hours later, when the doctor had been and Auld Slowey's body had been taken to the City Mortuary, Ann sank into a chair, exhausted.

'Thank you, John. My father was right - you are a good man. I hope you'll help me tell the men in the workshop about his death. Then we have to make plans for the future. I want to keep the workshop going if I can and I know my father trusted you to help me.'

'I'll gladly do anything I can, Ann.' John left, feeling a little relieved. *Maybe things would not be as bad as they had seemed earlier.*

20

December 1878

In Quarrier's Village, ice covered the pathways and garden areas. Six houses had been completed and almost two hundred children now lived there. As they emerged in the late afternoon from lessons, their breath turned into clouds in the freezing air. Tilly walked between Jane and Lizzie, holding tightly onto them. A group of boys pushed past.

'Oot the road, slowcoaches.' Their boots clattered on the ice as they ran and slid along the pathway.

'Can we go back to the house - I can't walk any further,' said Tilly, her voice trembling. They carefully made their way to the large house that was now their home. Mr Brown was throwing salt on the stairs leading to the house. He frowned when he saw them.

'What are you doing back? You know you're supposed to walk twice round the village for exercise before you come home for tea.' Tilly shrank back as his tall frame towered over them, and Jane spoke for her.

'Tilly's boot slips on the ice, so she can't walk.' Mr Brown sighed.

'Right. You come in, Tilly. Walk around the dormitory to get your legs moving. And don't forget I can hear you clumping about, so I'll know if you stop. Don't have me coming to check on you. You two carry on with your exercise.'

Jane and Lizzie set off. Pathways were in place around the houses, and shapes of streets were beginning to appear. Some even had names on boards dug into the gardens: Hope Avenue; Faith Avenue; Praise Road. Building work was continuing even on this cold winter's day. New workshops where the boys could learn joinery were in progress as well as a new laundry for the girls. There was even talk of a real school being built soon, as well as a church. Boys and girls were in separate groups for lessons and they lived in different houses, but saw each other outside. In this weather, everyone kept moving to keep warm but the ground was too slippery for games. As groups passed each other on the pathways, it almost seemed like being in an ordinary town, but they could only walk around the houses. There were no shops or stalls with people selling their wares; there were no animals; there were no carriages. Although at first they seemed to have more freedom, being allowed out of the house, they all knew now there was nowhere to go. High walls surrounded the village and the main gate was locked unless workers needed to get out or in. Jane knew she should feel lucky but her heart ached to be back in Glasgow with her family. Mrs Brown was kind enough and made sure they were fed, but she wasn't like real family. At church services, the children were told to thank God for their good fortune. Each time, Jane prayed that she would see John and Ellen and James soon. She felt sure she would rather be hungry with them than well fed with strangers.

'Jane. Lizzie. Wait for me. They stopped and Mary caught up.
'Where's Tilly?'
'Back at the house. Her boot was slipping.'
'She's lucky. It's freezing out here.' A group of boys were coming towards them.
'Seen red-haired Billy anywhere?'
'No, said Mary. Billy was a friendly boy that Jane had spoken to a few times. Like her, he was missing his family. He had been put in Cessnock Home when his father died and his mother was ill after having his little sister. He had been caught begging on the streets and was taken to the Home instead of prison because he was only eight. He had not seen his mother or sister again.

'I saw him coming out of class,' said Lizzie, 'but I don't know where he went.'

The boys walked away and the girls started back to the house, desperate to get out of the cold and the darkness which was falling. Mrs Brown met them at the door. 'In quickly, girls. Food will be on the table in five minutes. Put boots straight into the cloakroom - I don't want muck and ice all over my clean floor.' Girls were already making their way into the dining-room. Jane went and helped Tilly down the stairs from the dormitory. Mrs Brown said Grace, then they hungrily ate broth and bread with hot milk to follow. Suddenly a loud knocking was heard at the front door. They heard Mr Brown's voice saying, 'What's up?' and a man's voice replying, 'Young Billy Faulds is missing. Search your house in case he's hiding here, then join me at the Central Building to search the grounds.'

Mrs Brown came to ask, 'Anyone seen Billy Faulds anywhere after leaving school?' No-one had. They heard Mr and Mrs Brown opening and closing doors, then Mr Brown hurried out. 'I hope Billy's not sick or hurt,' said Jane. When all the dishes were done, the girls were allowed to read or chat in the big sitting-room for an hour before bed. Everyone was talking about the missing boy. At evening prayers, Jane prayed for Billy to be well.

Next morning on the way to lessons, Billy's friends still did not know where he was. The House Fathers and the builders were calling his name all over the village. As the children came out of class at dinner-time, a loud bell was ringing at the main gate of the village. This usually meant workers were coming in, but not at this time. Jane saw Mr Brown come out of the house and run to the gate. A few minutes later, Mr Alexander came driving a horse-drawn cart up towards one of the houses, the one where Jane knew Billy lived. Mr Brown was in the back of the cart, bent over a small, blanket-covered shape. The children looked on anxiously. 'Clear the pathways and get inside for dinner.' House Mothers and Fathers shooed them into houses.

At dinner, Lizzie asked Mrs Brown,

'What's happened to Billy?'

'I cannae tell ye yet, but we'll find out soon enough what mischief he's been up to, silly boy. On the way back to lessons, Jane saw some other boys from Billy's house. She called to the oldest one, Arthur,

'Where has Billy been? Is he sick?'

'We've been told not to talk about it.' He came closer and whispered, 'I heard our House Mother say they needed to get a doctor. He was found in a ditch beside the road. His leg's hurt and he has a bad cough. They think he's been out all night.' Jane was horrified, thinking how cold it had been the night before. She remembered Billy saying each time they spoke how much he wanted to go home. 'If they won't take me, I'll find my own way back. I'm not staying here,' he had told her. The afternoon seemed very long. When they were finally dismissed, the girls began their usual walk round the village. Down near the gate, workmen on ladders were cutting off the branches of a large tree beside the wall. When the girls stopped to look, one called out, 'Aye, well might you look. There'll be no more of you climbing up this tree to get out.'

*   *   *   *   *

Billy Faulds was not seen outside for a few days. The other boys from his house said he had been in bed for a day then was allowed up but only to stay in the house. At the next Sunday service, Jane saw him limping to a seat. His leg was bandaged and he seemed stooped over. During the service, the minister reminded them again of how lucky they were that God had led them to Mr Quarrier's Cottage Homes. 'You all have lovely houses to live in with caring House-parents. By next year we hope you will have a proper school and church, and twice as many young people living here. Be grateful for the education and training you are receiving which will prepare you for the day when you must make your own way in the world, but that day has not yet come. Bow your heads now and thank the Lord for the gifts he has given you and never forget what miserable lives you led before.'

Outside, the children met in groups for their walk before dinner. Jane saw Billy going slowly along the pathway and called to him. As he turned, she could see his hands were badly scratched, no doubt from climbing the branches of the tree he had used to try to escape, but his face was also bruised around his eye and cheek.

'Och, Billy, I'm sorry you were hurt. Did you land on your head when you went over the wall?'

'No, I cut my hands on the tree but I was fine. I started walking towards Bridge of Weir, hoping to sneak onto a train, but when it got dark I heard a cart coming behind me and I tried to hide. I fell in a ditch and cut my leg. Then it was hard to walk and I had to sleep in the ditch. I was caught the next day by Mr Alexander and he brought me back.'

'But the bruises on your face, how did they happen?'

'That was from my caring House Father as a punishment for the trouble I caused. I hate him now.' Jane was shocked at his poor face and at the anger and sadness in Billy's voice.

'As soon as my leg's better, I'm going to find another way to get out. I want to go home.'

'I'd like to go too, but I don't have a home to go to. I need to wait for my brother to come for me.' Even as she said this, Jane thought about how often she had talked about John coming for her, and wondered if he ever would. She walked slowly with Billy to his cottage, then went to hers.

21

Several months had passed since Auld Slowey's death. Ann was running the workshop well, to the surprise of the older men who worked there. Jimmy often remarked, 'Aye, she's proved me wrong. You were right about her, John.' She really missed her father - but enjoyed being in charge. She had always looked after the 'books', the business accounts, but was now often on the workshop 'floor' too, where the shoes and boots were made. At first, workers were reluctant to take orders from her, especially the men, but they soon came to realise that she knew the business well and their jobs depended on her keeping the factory open. John was now chief assistant and helped supervise the workers when Ann was working in the office. In the evenings, John would come and sit with her. They blethered for hours. They talked of their parents, discovering that Ann's father had come from Monaghan, a town in Ireland not far from Fermanagh where John's mother had lived. Ann's mother had come from Edinburgh, again not far from where John's father had been born. Like John, Ann had never been out of Glasgow and could only imagine their parents' lives before they arrived there.

On Sundays, John and Ann would go out walking in the streets or on the Green. Once, as they sheltered under a tree from a rain shower, Ann said,

'I'm very grateful to you, John, for everything you do for me. I hope you don't wish you were working somewhere else and feel you've got to stay with me. I know you promised my father, but you've looked after me and now I'm managing fine.'

'I love working with you and staying here. Once I can afford to, I'd like to get a room of my own, so that I could get Jane home, but there's nowhere else I'd want to be working. If I had my own room, you could come and visit me. I'm sure you'd like Jane.'

'If she's anything like you, I know I would.' John's heart pounded. He'd come to love Ann - but didn't dare hope that she felt the same.

'So you like me, then? That's nice to know.'

'Of course I do. You're like my friend and family. I'd really miss you if you left.'

'No need to worry about that, then.' Impulsively, he cuddled her and kissed the top of her head. She blushed.

'Thank you, John. I feel reassured now about the future.' When the rain finally stopped they left the Green, holding hands and smiling. The sun had come out again and life seemed full of promise as they strolled back to Schipka Pass.

22

Jane and Tilly walked slowly round the village in the Spring sunshine; they could see the River Gryffe sparkling and this pleasant view should have made them feel happy, but Jane's heart was heavy.

'I wonder if the River Clyde is sparkling today. I'd like to be walking there instead of here.'

'I know, Jane, but it's better than sleeping in a close where nobody sees the sun, or out on the street where it's cold and dirty. And we're getting food and lessons.' Jane nodded. She knew this was the truth, but she couldn't stop longing to go home. She tried and tried not to think about her family; then when she did, and couldn't clearly remember their faces, she felt guilty and scared. She wished she was brave like Billy Faulds and could run away, but what was the use? Billy had tried again to escape after the first time. He had hidden himself under the cart that took the workers back to town at the end of the day. Out on the road, he had fallen off and the wheel of the cart had run over him. The children were taken to the Hall next morning and told by Reverend Blackwell, one of their teachers, that Billy had died. 'Let this be a warning to all of you. Billy has gone to the Lord, but not in the way he should have done. It is God's will that you should be here, safe from evil, till another place is found for you. We already have many children who have gone to good homes or are working in jobs they could never have hoped to get before Mr Quarrier took them in. Be grateful and patient - your turn will come.' That night, Jane wept bitterly for Billy. She wondered if his mother knew that he had died trying to get home to her. There was no more talk of running away.

The number of children - and houses for them - had grown in the previous months. A proper schoolhouse was being built, and a huge laundry so that the girls could continue training for domestic work. The boys would be trained in joinery in huge sheds already in place. The gardens throughout the village were now covered in grass and flowers and had benches. Jane tried to forget the sadness in her life and concentrate on being happy here. 'Look. There's Mary and Lizzie waiting for us', said Tilly. The girls were sitting on the grass in the garden of their house. They were picking tiny flowers, white daisies and yellow buttercups, and making them into chains; carefully they made holes in the stems with their fingernails and fed the next stem through. Jane and Tilly joined in, and soon they were hanging them round each other's necks and laughing at the sight. They didn't notice a carriage stopping in front of the house till its shadow fell across them. As they looked up, a woman climbed out.

'It's Miss Mathieson from the Home,' said Mary. Miss Mathieson spoke to the driver, then went into the house, paying no attention to the girls.

'Maybe new girls are coming to live here,' said Jane. They watched the driver climb down and open the carriage door, but, instead of other children, he started bringing out wooden trunks and carrying them into the house. Soon, Miss Mathieson came out and climbed back into the carriage. The girls watched as it made its way further on and stopped outside one of the houses where the boys lived; more trunks were taken in. Again, Miss Mathieson got back into the carriage, but this time they saw it disappear towards the main gate. The door opened and Mrs Brown called to them, 'Come in and wash your hands before dinner, girls.' As they filed past her, she added, 'And get those weeds you're wearin' thrown away. It's hard enough keepin' you clean as it is.' The trunks they'd seen being brought in were lined along the hallway and Mr Brown was carrying them upstairs one by one.

When the girls were at the table eating dinner, Mrs Brown joined her husband in a storage room at the back of the house.

'Well, these look sturdy enough for the journey they've to make', she remarked.

'Aye, they do that. When will we know who'll be using them?'

'Mr Galbraith will send word soon, but Miss Mathieson said to expect a list of twenty boys and twenty girls. Others are going from James Morrison Street. We've to take delivery of clothes to fill the trunks over the next few weeks. Then we'll be told a departure date.

'Ah, well, not too long then.' He closed and locked the storage room and they went downstairs for dinner.

23

'You're quiet, John. Is something wrong?' John and Ann were holding hands as they walked on the Green, but John seemed preoccupied.

'Sorry, Ann. I was just thinking how close by my sister Jane is in the Home, yet she seems so far away because I'm not allowed to see her. I wish I had the means to take her out.'

'You will one day, John; I know it, and I'm looking forward to meeting her when that happens.' John hesitated, thinking how much closer the two of them had become recently - like a real couple - but not wanting to presume that Ann loved him as much as he loved her. He stopped and turned her towards him.

'It's not just that. I think you know how fond of you I am. I'd like us to be married, Ann, but I don't feel I've anything to offer you.'

'But there's nothing I need you to offer me except yourself. I'd like nothing better than to be your wife. You already support me in every way possible. I only feel lonely when you leave at night to go back downstairs. If we were married, I'd never feel like that again.'

'Oh, Ann, I've wished so long to hear that.'

'We could continue to stay at Schipka Pass. Nothing could be simpler.'

'I wonder if Ellen could take Jane again, but I know it would be a struggle for her. I don't even know if she's back home yet. Henry was quite unpleasant the last time I asked about her.'

'I won't hear of it, John. I know you want to keep your promise to Jane. She could come to us, couldn't she?'

'You have a heart of gold, Ann. It's no wonder I love you.' He cuddled her and kissed her, his heart pounding. She couldn't stop smiling.

'We'll be a family; when we have children of our own, Jane can help us with them. Why don't you go to Quarrier's and tell them our plans?'

'They told me not to return till I had somewhere for Jane to live with me. That won't be till we're married.'

'Then let's make that soon. I have no family to consider, so we can make our own arrangements.' John felt his heart racing. He'd never felt so happy.

'We can speak to Father Carmichael tomorrow after Mass', he said. That evening, they began to plan their life together.

'We can have my father's old room. I've already packed his things away (he didn't have much of his own), so Jane can have my room. Theresa can still have the recess bed in the kitchen.'

'I'll work hard for you, Ann. The money I save in rent can help buy food for the three of us.'

'We'll be fine; I know we will, John.'

'Jane will be a good help too. She'll need to go to school during the day - it's now the law- but she can help Theresa in the evenings. She's a good child and I'm sure you'll come to love her as I do.'

The next day, John and Ann went to Mass at Saint Mary's. As they were leaving, Father Carmichael, the Parish Priest, was standing at the top of the church steps saying goodbye to his parishioners, shaking hands with adults and patting their children gently on the head. He was white-haired and kindly-looking. They waited till they were the only ones left, then John said nervously,

'Good afternoon, Father. We'd like to speak to you about getting married here, quite soon if we can.'

'I see. Come into the sacristy and I'll take your details.' They followed him back through the church and into a large room off it.

'I know your faces, but you'll need to give me your names and other particulars.' When they had done this, and he had written them in a huge book, he said,

'The earliest I could marry you would be a month from now, the seventeenth of May, which will be the fourth Saturday coming, at ten o'clock. I have to put your names up at the back of the church for three weeks, saying you intend to marry. This is called posting your banns. If anyone knows of any reason why you can't marry, they have time to tell me before the ceremony. On the day, you will need two witnesses to your marriage. Come with them in time for ten o'clock Mass. God bless you till then.'

'Thank you, Father. God bless you.' Ann could hardly contain her excitement as they returned home.

'A month seems a long way away, but we have a lot to do. I'll ask Theresa to be my witness. Who will you have?'

'I'll ask Harry. He's the closest I have to a friend. I'd love our James to be there but he's still at sea.'

'As long as we're there, that's the important thing,' laughed Ann, her eyes twinkling with happiness.

24

Jane looked out of the schoolroom window at the May sunshine. She enjoyed lessons, but longed to be outside. The daily walk round the village was more pleasant now that winter was over, and she could play in the garden later with her friends. They still couldn't leave the village - but it was better than being in the Glasgow Home, with only the back yard for escape. Just then, a girl entered and passed a long piece of paper to the teacher, Reverend Blackwell. He read it over quickly. 'The following girls are to go to the Hall before going back to your Houses. I will come with you.' Jane's heart sank when her name was called, but at least Lizzie's and Mary's names were called too.

When the lesson ended, everyone else left, with Tilly whispering to Jane as she passed, 'I'll wait for you outside'. In the Hall were boys and girls from other classes. Reverend Blackwell called for silence, then said, 'Well, boys and girls. What wonderful news I have for you all. You have been selected to sail soon with Mr and Mrs Quarrier to Canada, where new homes and families will be found for you.' Jane's heart began to beat as if it would burst out of her chest. She recalled Mrs Brown's conversation with Miss Mathieson that she and Lizzie had overheard the day they arrived. She wanted to raise her hand or speak, but it was as if she was paralysed. All around her, girls and boys were chattering and some were calling out, 'When, Reverend Blackwell?' and 'Where is Canada?' Lizzie was saying, 'Maybe we'll see Kate there.' Reverend Blackwell raised his hand. 'I know this is exciting news and you will hear more about your trip in the coming days. Your House Mothers and Fathers already have trunks for you; inside them are clothes that good Christian people have provided for you so that you will start out well in your new lives. Let us now say the Lord's Prayer in thanks for your good fortune before you return to your Houses to eat.'

Jane could hear everyone pray as if from a distance. She could not utter a word. When the prayer was over, boys and girls moved towards the door. Jane's feet were leaden - she could not move. When she was the last child in the Hall, Reverend Blackwell came to her.

'Why, Jane, you look quite overcome.'

'Sir... I... I... think there's a mistake', she stammered. 'I can't go to Canada. I have to wait here for my brother or sister to come for me.'

'I'm sure you're the one who is mistaken, Jane. Children have been very carefully selected for their suitability. If what you're saying is true, your name wouldn't have been on the list, so go back to your House now and be grateful for this wonderful opportunity you've been given. No more of this nonsense.' Jane walked out of the building as if in a trance. Outside, Lizzie and Mary were waiting with Tilly, who was in tears.

'I don't want you all to go without me. Why am I not going?'

'I don't want to go at all. I can't. I won't,' said Jane and her tears came then - loud, raw sobs bursting from her throat.

'Come back to the house - maybe Mrs Brown will help,' said Lizzie. Mrs Brown was waiting at the door. 'Inside quickly, you girls: your food's getting cold.' When she saw Jane and Tilly crying, she pulled them aside.

'What on earth is going on? Have you two been fighting?' Through her tears, Tilly gulped,

'Reverend Blackwell says Jane's going to Canada. I want to go with her, but she doesn't want to go.'

'We'll deal with this when you've eaten. Don't let precious food go to waste - you should know better. Wash your hands and faces and get to the table!' Jane could barely eat, but forced down some broth and bread. The cold milk soothed her burning throat. When the tables were cleared, Mrs Brown took Jane and Tilly aside. She spoke to Tilly first.

'Tilly, you must remember your short leg and how slow it makes you. The work the others are going to do in Canada would be too hard for you. You'll get a job here one day that you can manage.'

'But I don't want to be here without my friends.'

'It's not for you to decide, Tilly. How dare you question what Mr Quarrier has planned for you? Think where you'd be now if he hadn't taken you in - out on the streets with no-one looking after you, that's where.' Tilly's head fell forward and she wept, sniffling onto her sleeve.

'And you, Jane. What do you mean, you don't want to go? After the care that has been taken of you and the money that has been spent on you? It's time to give something back, let some other poor beggar have your place here. Mr and Mrs Quarrier would be very hurt if they heard of this, and I'll be forced to tell them if it doesn't stop. D'ye hear me?'

'But Reverend Millar said Mr Galbraith would tell my brother John if I was moving, so that he can find me. He'll be coming soon, I'm sure.'

'Well, you've to go back to the Glasgow Home before the ship sails. You can speak to Mr Galbraith there if you dare. In the meantime, pray to the good Lord for guidance. He always acts in your best interests. Now go, the two of you, and mend your ungrateful ways!'

That evening, after prayers in the House, Mrs Brown spoke to all her girls about the forthcoming move to Canada. 'Those of you going should feel very fortunate. You'll be going to families who want you. In return, you'll help with household duties just as you usually would. You'll be able to go to school, attend church and thrive in a beautiful new country. Mr and Mrs Quarrier will be travelling with you, so you'll be perfectly safe on the journey.' She told them that those not chosen this time should not be disappointed – there might be other opportunities. If not, they would no doubt find work in Scotland when it was time to leave the village. 'This is what you're being trained for every day in our kitchens and laundries and school lessons. Remember Mr Quarrier in your prayers each day and give thanks that you've been rescued from the miserable lives that you had. Go now – it'll soon be time for bed.' In the bathroom, as they washed for bed, Jane looked at Tilly's face and saw her own misery reflected there. She whispered, 'We'll talk in bed. Try and stay awake for a while.' Tilly nodded.

Once upstairs, when the dormitory door had been locked for the night, Jane lay and tried to imagine her future. She hadn't wanted to come to Quarrier's Village, but now she would happily stay. *If only she could hear from John or Ellen.* Soon, heavy breathing, snores and snuffles meant the other girls were sleeping. Jane crept out of bed and tiptoed to Tilly's bedside. Like Jane, she was wide awake. She moved over and Jane climbed in beside her. The two held hands and tried not to cry.

'What will happen to me if you all go?' whispered Tilly. 'I'll have no-one to help me.'

'Mr and Mrs Brown will make sure someone helps you.'

'I don't like Mr Brown. He says horrible things to me when I have to stay in by myself. He's like my stepfather.' She wiped a silent tear off her cheek.

'Oh, Tilly. I wish I could stay with you. I don't want to go.'

'What'll you do?'

'I'm going to speak to Mr Galbraith in Glasgow when we go there. He might get a message to John. He might just send me back here - then I'll be able to look after you.'

'Oh, Jane, I hope so. I know you want to go back to your family, but I'm sure they'll come one day, and they know you're here.'

'I hope so too, Tilly. I'll try my best. I'd better go back to bed - I don't want to get into any more trouble with the Browns.' She kissed Tilly gently on the forehead as she remembered her mother used to do to her, then slid carefully onto the floor.

As she began to tiptoe across the room, someone cried out and Jane hurried into bed. There was another louder cry and she could see someone's arms waving. It was Sarah, a girl they knew from the Orphan Home. The girl sat up, swayed, then fell out of bed with a loud thump. Jane and Tilly went to her side. She was rolling around on the floor and moaning.

'I think she's sick,' said Tilly. 'What'll we do?'

'If we make a noise, Mrs Brown will come.' Jane ran to the door, banged on it and called out,

'Mrs Brown. Come quickly. Sarah's sick.' Other girls began to wake and some joined Jane in knocking on the door and calling for help. As they heard the lock turn, they hurried back to bed, leaving Jane alone.

'What's this noise about? Jane Anderson, you'd better not be making a fuss about Canada again or I'll make you sorry you spoke.'

'Sarah's sick. She fell out of bed.' Mrs Brown looked at Sarah and quickly called downstairs for her husband to bring a lamp. She knelt beside Sarah and felt her forehead, shaking her head. When Mr Brown arrived, she took the lamp. In its light, Sarah's skin looked red and damp with sweat as she thrashed about. 'Quick. Carry her downstairs. We'll need to send for the doctor. The rest of you – back to sleep at once.' Mr Brown scooped Sarah up and they left, locking the door behind them.

Jane went back to bed and thought about what she would say to Mr Galbraith when she saw him.

25

Sarah lay on an armchair in the kitchen. Mrs Brown had covered her with a blanket to try to stop her shivering. The heat from the kitchen stove brought the sweat pouring from the girl's forehead. She still seemed asleep but was mumbling and moaning. 'Try to lie still, Sarah; the doctor'll be here soon.' Heating on the stove was a pan of onions and one of water. Mrs Brown stirred the onions then poured them into a dish. She sat this outside the back door to cool. She poured some hot water into a bowl and added some balsam from a bottle in the cupboard, then she sat the bowl on a small table beside Sarah. She moved the feverish child to the side of the armchair so that the steam from the bowl rose up around her face. 'There now, that will help you breathe. I'll be back in a minute.' When she returned, she was holding a pair of stockings. She fetched the dish of onions from outside and began spooning the onions into them. Then she lifted back the blanket and carefully put the stockings on Sarah's feet, pulling them up tight to hold them on. She lifted a cloth from the line above the stove, wiped Sarah's face and held the bowl of steaming water closer to the girl's face. Suddenly, a violent cough wracked Sarah's body and she coughed up yellow mucus. Mrs Brown wrinkled her nose but wiped it away. Sarah's eyes opened, shining and watery - she looked wildly round the room for a moment then closed them once more.

The door opened and Mr Brown appeared with a man carrying a leather bag.

'Doctor Sim, thank you for coming. This is Sarah. I've put onion poultices on her feet and let her breathe some balsam in water. She has begun to cough up mucus from her chest, so my remedies are working, I think.'

'Thank you, Mrs Brown; you have done well, but let me have a look at her now.' He opened Sarah's eyelids and her eyes rolled in their sockets. Her hands came out from under the blankets and she tried to push him away. In the lamplight, shadows round the wall looked like many ghostly arms waving. Rolling from side to side, Sarah tried to speak but nothing she said made sense. Doctor Sim shook his head.

'She is showing signs of a chest infection. You have stopped it from worsening, Mrs Brown, but I fear she needs to go to hospital. We must remove her from the other children in case the infection spreads to them.' Mr and Mrs Brown looked at each other anxiously.

'She is meant to be going to Canada in a few days. Could she not stay here and get better?'

'I'm sorry, that is out of the question. She's unlikely to be cured in a few days, and even if she improved, if she went on a ship and got worse again, the spread of what she has would be a disaster. I'll take her with me now and try to get her into a hospital. It's a pity the infirmary here in the village has not been completed. God willing, it will be soon. Help me out to the carriage with the child, Mr Brown. Hopefully, her removal now will save other children.' As Mr Brown carried Sarah, wrapped tightly in the blanket, Mrs Brown took a small pouch from a drawer in the kitchen dresser. Coins rattled as she passed it to Doctor Sim.

'I'm obliged to you, Doctor. I'm sorry you were disturbed during the night and now have extra work to do. I'll let Mr Quarrier know what you've said.' Doctor Sim touched his hat and nodded.

'No matter. Such is the work that must be done. We live in difficult times.' He lifted his bag and followed Mr Brown outside. When her husband returned, Mrs Brown sighed and said,

'What'll we do now about Canada? This has happened at the worst possible time. Can we send someone in her place?'

'Sending that pest Tilly would help us all. She has been such a misery since she heard her friends were being sent away without her, moping and grumbling at every turn. I'd rather not have to deal with her after they go. She tries my patience sorely.'

'I still think her short leg could be a problem, but she's roughly the same size as Sarah, so the clothes in the trunk would do her. Miss Mathieson arrives tomorrow and we can ask her then. Bed for us now - we'll be up again in a few hours.' She closed the door of the stove and lifted the oil-lamp to light their way upstairs.

At breakfast, the others noticed that Sarah was missing. Lizzie asked Mrs Brown where she was. 'The doctor took her to hospital as she has a chest infection. She'll be back when she's better. Now the rest of you, eat up and drink your milk. We don't want anyone else getting sick - Sarah has cost Mr Quarrier a lot of money.' The rest of the girls ate quietly then went to their classes.

When Miss Mathieson arrived later in the afternoon, Mrs Brown told her about Sarah and how the doctor had said she could not sail to Canada. Miss Mathieson raised her hand to her mouth.

'That is most inconvenient at this late stage. I'm staying here this evening and taking the children to Glasgow tomorrow to board ship, so I can't get word to Mr Quarrier.' Mrs Brown glanced briefly at her husband.

'Miss Mathieson, we have thought of a possible solution. Young Tilly has been upset at not being chosen, seeing as how her close friends are all going. We wondered if she could replace Sarah. It would save losing the place on the ship.'

'Isn't she the one with paralysis and a short leg?'

'Yes, but she was fitted with a new boot to even up the leg, and now gets about quite well.'

'Does she attend to all her duties in the House like the others?'

'Oh, yes, with no difficulty, and she is really keen to go.'

'I see. We normally cannot send children with health problems but if she is fit to work it might be possible. I'll take her to Glasgow with the others and if Mr Quarrier is against the idea, I'll bring her back with your new arrivals. Thank you for the suggestion. Now, Mr Brown, can we have the girls' trunks brought down, please? I have a bible to put in each one.'

When the girls returned from school, the trunks were lined up in the hallway. Each had a label with a name written on it. Miss Mathieson took Tilly aside.

'Tilly, you know Sarah can't go to Canada because she is ill?'

'Yes, Miss.'

'Mr and Mrs Brown have kindly suggested that you go in her place. This is not my decision to make, but you will come to Glasgow with me tomorrow and Mr Quarrier will decide. Nothing is certain and you may well have to return here. Do you understand?' Tilly's eyes shone with excitement.

'Oh, yes, Miss. Thank you, Miss.' At dinner, she told her friends. Lizzie and Mary hugged her, and Jane said, 'I'm happy for you, Tilly. I still don't want to go, but you'll have Lizzie and Mary. I'll miss you all when I go home to my family, but I'll be glad you're all together.'

After evening prayers, Miss Mathieson called for the girls going to Canada, including Tilly, to meet her in the hallway. As they clustered around her, she said, 'Here are your trunks for the journey. I want you to find the one with your name on the label.' When they had all found their trunks, she continued, 'Inside you should have two sets of clothing and an extra pair of boots. You'll also have a bible. All of these precious things have been provided by good, Christian people for your move to Canada. If you make sure you read your bible every day, the good Lord will always be with you. We will leave for Glasgow after breakfast tomorrow, so go to bed now and sleep well.'

In bed, Jane lay for a long time, practising over and over what she would say to Mr Galbraith. If she could even stay in Glasgow, near John and Ellen, she felt sure she would make it home one day. Maybe, like Tilly, some other girl would go to Canada in her place. In the morning, she was pale and tired. When the carriages arrived to take them to the station in Bridge of Weir, and Miss Mathieson told them all to thank Mr and Mrs Brown for looking after them, Jane couldn't speak a word.

The train journey to Glasgow seemed all too short. Everyone else was talking about what Canada would be like - Jane didn't care. When they arrived at St. Enoch's Station, carriages were waiting for them. As they passed through the streets, thronged with people and horses, Jane felt she was almost home already. It seemed such a long time since she had been here. *If only she could see Ellen or John in the street and shout to them.* She imagined them running to pick her up and take her home. She wondered what Ellen's children looked like now. *After all she had learned in Quarrier's Homes, she could be a good help to them now. She needed to be brave and polite when she spoke to Mr Galbraith and, surely, he would let her stay.* Into this daydream burst Miss Mathieson's voice, 'We have arrived, girls. Climb down quickly, please, and follow me inside.' As Jane got down and looked up at the James Morrison Street Home, it seemed to

loom over her threateningly, and she was suddenly cold inside with
fear.

26

Inside the Home, all was hustle and bustle - the staircase full of boys and girls; the hallway full of adults, talking and laughing loudly. 'Straight to the upstairs Hall, children.' Jane's group joined the others and went upstairs. In the Hall, large tables were laid out with bread, pastries, jugs of milk and pots of tea. 'Line up against the wall. Mr Quarrier and his guests will be arriving shortly, then you can go and eat. Your trunks are being taken to the ship and will be waiting for you there.' Miss Mathieson moved towards the door and Jane ran from her line to stop her before she left.

'Miss Mathieson, can I speak to Mr Galbraith, please?'

'Today on this busiest of days, Jane? What on earth for?' Jane stammered nervously,

'I don't want to go on the ship. I want to wait for my brother to come for me. Mr Galbraith said he would let him know if I was moving.'

'I'll be speaking to him about Tilly and will mention your concerns - but I doubt your arrangements can be changed now. Stand with the others and I'll come back soon.'

'Thank you, Miss.' While more children filed into the Hall, men and women in fine clothes arrived and sat in rows of seats laid out for them around small tables. Jane stood with Tilly, Mary and Lizzie, anxiously watching the door.

After what seemed like hours, Miss Mathieson returned and called to Jane and Tilly. She took them to a corner of the room where it was quiet. Jane felt sure everyone in the room could hear her heart beating against her ribs.

'I have spoken to Mr Galbraith, girls. Tilly, you are being allowed to go to Canada on the condition that you work hard wherever you are placed. Your leg should not hold you back from carrying out your duties without complaint. Miss Bilbrough in Canada will choose you a suitable family. You should be very grateful.'

'Thank you, Miss. I promise I'll work hard.'

'Now, Jane. Mr Galbraith cannot possibly speak to you today; he's far too busy with arrangements for the sailing. However, he has asked me to say that he wishes you to go to Canada as he feels this will be best for you. Your brother has had many months to find a place for you with him and this has not happened. Your brother placed you in Mr Quarrier's care and he has decided that Canada will provide a better life for you - with a new family who want you with them. We cannot keep you in our Homes when other children on the streets are desperate for a place here. Be reasonable, Jane, and stop this nonsense. Pray to God to make you brave and help you in your new life. Now, join the others. Mr Quarrier is on his way.'

'But Miss...'

'Enough, Jane. You have had your say and Mr Galbraith has had his. Think now of your marvellous future and do not mention this again. If your brother loves you, he'll want what's best for you, I'm sure.'

Jane walked to join her friends as if in a trance, her head full of Miss Mathieson's words. *John had had many months to come for her. Maybe he did want her to go to a new family and that was why he hadn't come for her. She didn't want to burden him or Ellen. Maybe, with a job, she could save money and come back one day. For now she had no choice.* She rejoined Tilly, who was happily sharing her good news with Lizzie and Mary. They were delighted that Jane was going too.

Mr Quarrier entered the room. 'Good day, everyone and thank you for coming. We don't have much time - we have to be aboard in time to sail this afternoon. The sun is out to bless our journey on this momentous day, the fourteenth of May in the year of our Lord, 1879 - a day when our young orphans' lives will change forever. It is thanks to many of you that they can go, so I wanted you to share in their send-off. These fortunate children will soon be settled in a new country with new families, but neither they nor I will forget your generosity. Be assured that your efforts are leading to a better society in Scotland, particularly here in Glasgow where many children suffer poverty and the neglect that comes with it. Let's all say The Lord's Prayer in thanks.' Mr Quarrier led it. Jane couldn't speak and risk crying. He then went on to direct guests to seats around the Hall. As the children left the room, servants moved forward with tea-pots and plates of pastries.

Downstairs, the children ate their last meal in Glasgow. When they had finished, Miss Mathieson said, 'Now line up and make your way to the front door. There are omnibuses waiting to take you to the ship.' Outside, several huge carriages with doors and windows waited. At the front of each, a man held the horses' reins. Staff from the Home helped the excited children up into their seats, then they climbed to seats on top. Jane scanned the people standing on the pavement, in case Mr Galbraith would come to take her off, but he was nowhere to be seen. She thought of the night she had arrived with John and couldn't believe what had happened to her since then. *How long would it be till she could come back?*

27

When everyone was settled, the Quarrier family and an unfamiliar, young woman, all in smart clothes, took the lead in a smaller carriage. The procession set off amidst cheers, waves and applause from the onlookers. They proceeded down James Morrison Street and along the Broomielaw. There were throngs of people on the cobbled pathways, some pushing barrows filled with goods of every description. The masts of the many ships berthed there bobbed back and forth in the May sunlight. All too quickly for Jane, the carriages trundled to a halt and the children were helped down onto the quayside. The young woman from Mr Quarrier's carriage came to arrange them in a line, each child beside a partner; her voice could be heard above the noise all around them. 'I'm Miss Sliman. I'll be with you on the journey so follow me closely. Keep away from the edge of the quayside - we don't want to lose anyone.'

She led them through the crowds. Tilly was holding tightly onto Jane's arm, trying not to slip on the cobbles. Miss Sliman stopped in front of a huge ship with a wooden pathway and a railing leading from the quay to the ship. 'Stop now. Carefully climb this gangplank and give your names to the officer waiting at the top.' As they waited to board, Jane could see a name on the side of the ship. *S.S. Nestorian.* She sounded it out to take her mind off the future. 'Nest...or...i...an.' *Maybe it would be like a nest and keep them safe like birds.* She hoped so, but in her heart she wished that she could fly away from here. Tilly, for once, was silent beside her. Behind them, Lizzie and Mary held hands nervously.

Climbing up the gangplank. Jane looked over the side and stared into the dirty, murky water of the Clyde. She had the feeling of being pulled towards it. Shivering then, she looked at the ship - close up it seemed even bigger. Long as a street and its masts higher than any building. *How would it stop from sinking when they all got on?* 'Move forward, please.' They gave their names to a man in uniform and were lifted onto the deck. Jane looked at the huge chains and ropes holding the ship to the quayside: everything seemed dangerous and frightening, but still Mr Quarrier smiled widely. 'Come along, children. Our adventure will soon begin.' Mrs Quarrier held her hat in place and walked among the children, straightening bonnets and capes and arranging them so that they were facing the quayside.

When they were all on board, Mr Quarrier called, 'Look - our friends in the new Salvation Army band have come to see us off. They'll play *Safe in the arms of Jesus* and we'll all sing along. You know it well; Miss Sliman will lead us.' He waved to a group of people in uniform who began playing shiny instruments and the children's voices rang out. A crowd had gathered behind the band; when the hymn was over, they applauded loudly. 'We have many friends here to wish us well, so wave them goodbye.' The smiling children waved and the crowd waved back.

A bell rang, a loud horn sounded and sailors hurried forward to reel in ropes and chains. The noise of it all filled the air, but then a louder, grinding noise began. 'Don't worry, children,' shouted Mr Quarrier, 'That's the engine starting up. You'll soon get used to it. Remember it's getting us to our destination - be thankful for it.' The ship moved off and the deck beneath their feet tilted from side to side. Jane and Tilly gripped each other. 'One more wave and we will go to our berths.' They waved as enthusiastically as they could, as the crowd on the quayside grew smaller.

Miss Sliman led them along the deck, behind structures like small houses - each had a door with a round window framed in shiny brass. Miss Sliman stopped at a staircase that disappeared down into the ship. 'I'll go first. Come behind me and hold on to the rails. You'll soon get used to the stairs but be very careful. In the gloom of another deck, sailors moved busily around, disappearing at times behind grey canvas curtains draped from ceiling to floor. Jane could hear Tilly whimpering as she struggled to keep her footing. They all proceeded down yet another staircase to the lowest deck. Oil lamps strung around the walls pierced the gloom with a yellow glow. 'Well done, children. We have reached the sleeping berths. Boys to the left and girls to the right.'

They were led into curtained-off areas where wooden frames stretched from floor to ceiling, forming bunks with high wooden sides. On each was a straw mattress in a cotton cover, with a folded blanket. In the middle of the room was a long table surrounded by stools nailed onto the floor. In one corner, buckets had been arranged under a plank with holes in it, to serve as a toilet – there was a curtain to pull round for privacy. Jane, Tilly, Lizzie and Mary stayed together and were given beds in the same area. Tilly quickly chose a bottom bunk and anxiously held on to the wooden frame. Jane took the next bottom bunk while Lizzie and Mary, laughing excitedly, climbed the ladders to the bunks above.

Milk was brought to them for supper. It was in small, metal cups which they had to hold tightly, to stop them from sliding along the table. With the noise of the ship's engine, conversation was impossible so the girls drifted away and lay down.

28

Jane awoke to the dull drone of the engine and the creaking of wood, struggling for a moment to remember where she was. Stiff from lying on the wooden bunk, tired from turning to get comfortable, she wondered if everyone had been kept awake. The unfamiliar motion of the ship had also made her feel sick in the night but now she wanted to get up and move around - wash the sleep and the bad night from her eyes. Above, she could hear Mary getting restless too. She turned and knelt up in a crackle of straw, putting first one leg then the other over the wooden side, holding on tightly to the frame for balance. Beneath her feet, she could clearly feel the ship's motion. *How could such a large object stay afloat?* From the next bunk, she could hear Tilly's voice. 'Jane, is that you? Can you help me get out? I'm scared I'll fall.' Her heavy boot lay at the bottom of her bunk, the other underneath. All around the room, girls were climbing warily out of bunks.

Miss Sliman arrived with a large jug of water and a bowl; Miss Quarrier brought towels and soap. They laid these out on a table behind a curtain. 'Use the toilet buckets then quickly have a wash. Keep your towel to use again, as you'll not get another.' Miss Sliman returned with a jug of milk and a pot of porridge. 'Sit at the table, girls. You can have breakfast then we'll go up on deck for some fresh air.' This sounded like a welcome release from the stench wafting through the room from the toilet buckets. Jane tried to ignore it as she ate.

Breakfast over, Miss Sliman led them up the steep stairs to the top deck. Jane climbed slowly, with Tilly holding onto her pinafore. Once on deck, they saw Mr and Mrs Quarrier looking out across the water. Land was appearing through the morning mist. Hills and trees and what looked like tiny houses were coming into view. The children went to look over the rails. 'Well timed, children. The land you can see is the Mull of Kintyre. This will be your last view of Scotland, so it'll be a nice memory to carry with you to your new homes.' It didn't look familiar; it wasn't full of people and buildings and animals like Glasgow: Jane didn't think she would remember it at all. 'It's a beautiful day, so have a walk around the deck, to help you find your sea legs. This evening, we'll be able to see Ireland; after that, the next land we see will be Canada.'

Jane and her friends began to walk around the deck: sailors were emptying toilet buckets over the ship's side into the sea - they hurried past in case the breeze would bring the night-soil back towards them. Further on, men were scrubbing the wooden deck and others were climbing the masts and working with ropes. It was a completely different world. And through it all, the ship heaved up and down in the grey, choppy water. The Mull of Kintyre soon disappeared from view, leaving the children milling around in groups, leaning over the rails to look into the water.

As the sun rose, the children relaxed and there was an air of nervous excitement. Jane and the others found a bench near one of the cabins.

'I wonder what Canada will be like', said Lizzie, 'and our new families. I hope mine like me.'

'I want brothers and sisters' sighed Mary, 'but I hope we'll still see each other a lot.' Tilly clapped her hands, smiling.

'If we're going to a village like Bridge of Weir, we'll be able to visit each other and play in the gardens. Maybe my new ma and da will get me new boots that I can run about in.' Their conversation was interrupted by a loud bell. Miss Sliman and Miss Quarrier came along the deck, calling, 'Everyone down to the first lower deck for dinner.'

Jane was hungry, but the sight of her soup swaying in her bowl and the feel of the ship moving beneath their feet made her feel ill. She tried to ignore that and gingerly swallowed some down. She noticed others were leaving their food unfinished. Miss Sliman walked around the tables trying to encourage them. 'Come along, children. You must eat to keep up your strength. You'll soon get used to the motion of the ship - it's perfectly normal.'

When everyone had eaten what they could, given their nausea, they were herded back upstairs onto the top deck. The Quarriers were pointing out across the water. 'Look, everyone. See that small island with a tall tower? That's called a lighthouse and its light warns ships to keep away from dangerous rocks. The island is Rathlin Island. Beyond that, the land you see is the coast of Antrim in Ireland. This is as close as we'll get to the mainland, then we reach the open sea.' Jane thought of her mother, Roseanne, who had come from Ireland to Glasgow many years before. *It was strange to think of her making the same journey as Jane in the opposite direction. Had she felt sick? Had she ever wanted to go back? She'd left her mother and father behind to seek a better life in Glasgow. How brave she'd been.* 'I'm going to try to be brave, Tilly.' Tilly squeezed her friend's arm. They watched till the Irish coast disappeared.

As the evening wore on, the sea grew wilder and darker. When daylight began to disappear, Mr Quarrier came along and called them to evening prayers on the middle deck. In the gloom of the lamplight, Jane could see how pale Tilly was.

'I'm feart, Jane. I cannae stay on ma feet.' Jane held her hand.

'I'm feart too but we'll be fine: just stay beside me.' Mr Quarrier led them in some brief prayers, then said,

'I'm sure you can feel the breeze getting stronger outside. It's nothing to worry about. However, Captain Henderson has advised us to remain in our sleeping quarters this evening. Food will be brought to you. Go carefully now and rest till morning.

The steps seemed steeper than before and the sway of the ship threw the children against those in front. They were glad to reach the sleeping quarters. They ate what they could of their food, before climbing wearily into their bunks. Miss Sliman came round to check that everyone was safely in bed. 'Sleep well. Tomorrow you will feel like little sailors, used to the rocking of the ship.'

29

All night, the ship rolled from side to side and up and down. In her
bunk, Jane held onto the wooden frame to stop herself from tossing
around, sleeping very little. Her stomach heaved, and throughout the
sleeping quarters, she could hear groaning and crying. In the morning,
Miss Quarrier came, looking pale and unsteady; she'd brought bread,
milk and a pot of porridge - the smell of it made Jane nauseous. 'Good
morning, children. I'm afraid Miss Sliman's unwell this morning - it's
been a rough night for us all and Captain Henderson recommends that
you stay in your quarters today, in bed if necessary, but try to eat
something.' She waited while the girls crept gingerly from their bunks,
then she carried on to the next sleeping area. Most, like Jane, refused
porridge but tried to eat a little bread. Jane felt she could barely chew,
and swallowing made her feel as if she was choking - she even tried
washing it down with some milk, but soon gave up and returned to her
bunk. Vomiting could be heard from the toilet area and she tried to
block out the sound. A young sailor came and left bowls by their beds.

'You can be sick in the bowls if you cannae make the bucket. We
don't want to scrub more planks than we have tae. The morra, the sea
should be calmer.'

'Will we be in Canada tomorrow?' Lizzie asked. He shook his
head, laughing.

'Ten days, if we're lucky.' He skipped up the stairs, unaffected by
the rolling of the ship.

Jane closed her eyes, trying to think of something nice - she
remembered Kate and how like a sister she had been. She still missed
her, sometimes looking around to catch sight of Kate's red curls before
remembering she'd gone. She thought about them making daisy chains
in the gardens at Bridge of Weir with their friends, in the sunshine. 'Do
you think Kate's journey to Canada was like this, Tilly?' From the next
bunk, she could hear Tilly moaning. 'Jane, I feel awfie sick - I need to go
to the toilet.' Jane climbed out of her bunk and went to her.

Together they struggled to put her heavy boot on. Tilly held
tightly onto Jane as they negotiated the trip to the toilet, which felt like

miles. Behind the curtain, the smell from the buckets enveloped them. Jane retched and vomited into the nearest one, while Tilly used another. They took turns at washing their hands and faces while they held each other steady. The water in the jug slopped from side to side and Jane tried not to think of what the sea must look like now. Back in bed, the effort to stay upright was too much, and they both lay down again. The noise of wood creaking throughout the ship was terrifying. At one point, Jane's bunk slid forward with a loud crack, separating from the ship's side. Terrified, Jane and Mary climbed in beside Tilly and Lizzie. The bunk seemed to settle again, but they stayed where they were, huddling together.

At midday, Miss Quarrier returned with dry biscuits and segments of oranges. 'Try to eat some biscuits, everyone. Suck the oranges to freshen your mouths.' She noticed Jane and Mary in the other bunks.

'You can't be comfortable there, girls. Why have you moved?'

'Our bunk broke, Miss. It's not attached now and we were feart it would fall.'

'I see. I'll let some of the crew know - they'll fix it. Don't worry.'

The day passed with no let-up in the weather. Tea-time came and went with very little food being eaten. Sailors changed the toilet buckets in the evening. The girls stayed in bed, hoping the night would pass quickly but Jane and Tilly made one more trip to the buckets, holding hands as they returned. They were warily trying to negotiate their way back, when a huge roll of the ship almost made them lose their footing. Looking up, they could see the broken bunk sliding towards them: it seemed enormous and the girls all around began to scream as they tried to move out of its path. With horror, they saw it topple; they almost made it to the other bunk, but Tilly stumbled and fell. Her hand slipped from Jane's and in seconds she had disappeared under the moving bunk. There was a sound of running feet as boys from the next sleeping area came to see what was happening. Together, boys and girls tried to lift the heavy bunk. Jane was weeping with dread and fear for her friend. One boy ran, shouting, to the deck above and crewmen rushed to help. Captain Henderson arrived with Mr Quarrier to find the children wailing, and called, 'Take these children away immediately to other quarters.'

As the sailors lifted the heavy bunk, they saw Tilly beneath it. She didn't move or make a sound and a stream of blood ran from her brow. The Captain bent over her, shaking his head. He whispered to Mr Quarrier, 'I fear we've lost her. I'll carry her up to the spare cabin that we use as an infirmary, but I doubt there is anything we can do.' The two men left, Tilly in the Captain's arms. Some of the crew set about re-attaching the bunk to the bulwark of the ship. Hearing the hammering, the children crept back to hear if Tilly was safe. Soon Miss Quarrier arrived, pale and dishevelled. 'Tilly's been taken to the ship's infirmary for medical attention. Let's all pray for her recovery and get back to our bunks. The broken one has been repaired.' After a brief prayer, the girls went back to bed and Jane climbed into Tilly's bunk where she felt closer to her friend. She prayed and prayed that Tilly would get better.

30

On Glasgow Green, John and Ann walked in the May sunshine. Theresa and Harry accompanied them from their marriage ceremony at Saint Mary's. The Green was a place they'd always felt happy in, but Ann also wanted to keep her dress and shoes clean - the grass was cleaner than the streets. John had made her new leather shoes for the wedding and the dress she was wearing had been her mother's wedding dress, cream silk with tiny pink roses embroidered round the neck and hem. A new veil for church and her outfit had been complete. John was wearing a jacket of Auld Slowey's, as was Harry; Theresa wore a good dress of Ann's and they all felt very smart strolling along. No-one would have guessed that they'd hardly spent anything on their outfits.

'Where are we going, Ann? What's the surprise?' asked Theresa.

'Well, Mrs Anderson, I think you should tell them now,' laughed John.

'We're going for a late breakfast to the Crown Luncheon Rooms in Argyle Street - the place Miss Kate Cranston opened last year.' Harry had hoped they were going to a public house, maybe Sloans, for a glass of beer, but breakfast would do nicely. Theresa's eyes widened.

'Will they let the likes of us in? I hear it's very posh, and business people go there.'

'John and I are business people now. Anyway, my father left me money for my wedding and that's where I want to go, even if we never go again.' John kissed Ann on the cheek.

'This is your special day, my dear - you may go where you please.' Secretly, he was relieved that he wasn't having to pay for breakfast - he'd been worrying about how they would celebrate their wedding, when Ann discovered a letter from her father, left in a large box with his wife's wedding dress. In it, he said he hoped Ann would marry a good man, and that she'd wear her mother's dress so that she would be with her in spirit on her wedding day, even though her mother had passed away many years before. With the letter was some money for Ann to use for this special day, a day that he must have realised he would never see. Ann had wept when she discovered the contents of the box. John knew she wouldn't tell the story now for fear of crying again, but he knew how much it had meant to her. The only thing that took away from his enjoyment of the day was that his family could not be there. 'My family will love you when you all meet', he whispered to his beautiful bride. His plan was to go to the Orphan Home next day to ask for Jane back, now that they had a home for her. He thought about how he would make the announcement, and could imagine her joy.

'I've even reserved a table. It's a beautiful place', Ann was telling Theresa and Harry.

When they left the Green, they walked to Argyle Street, admiring the lovely buildings commissioned by successful merchants in this ever-growing city. All around, horse-drawn carriages and people were dashing to and fro without a moment to spare. In the Luncheon Rooms, the atmosphere was suddenly calm: polished wood panelling glowed in the soft light from lamps on the walls - tables were covered with beautiful, white linen covers, and a candelabrum sat in the centre of each. Silver cutlery gleamed. The whole picture was reflected beautifully in stained glass windows around the room. Young women in black dresses with snowy white aprons and caps served well-dressed customers. As the wedding group entered the salon, a woman in a lavender-coloured gown came forward.

'Good day, ladies and gentlemen, may I help you?'

'We have a table reserved in the name of Anderson', said Ann.

'Ah, yes, of course. Please come this way.' They followed her to a table set for four, in a quiet corner. The stained glass behind it cast rainbow colours across the spotless cloth; a small brass bell sat on the corner of the table and a printed menu sat at each place.

'When you've chosen what you'd like to eat, ring the bell and one of the waitresses will take your order.' The lady in lavender swept back to her position at the door.

The four looked at each other in wonder and could not stop smiling.

'I can't believe I'm to be served at table', said Theresa. 'I'll have to stop myself from running into the kitchen to fetch the food.' The others laughed, and Ann rolled her eyes.

'You mustn't think of it. Please consider this a reward for all the years you've helped me, especially this morning. I don't know what I'd have done without you.'

'Thank you, too, Harry,' said John. I'm glad you're here with us. You've been a good friend to me.'

'And you to me. Congratulations, both of you - I hope you'll be very happy together.' Ann flushed with pleasure.

'Let's look at the menu. Choose anything you like.'

'Please let me ring the bell.' said Theresa, and they laughed delightedly. In the end, each had a hearty breakfast, followed by freshly-baked scones, and tea served in china cups. All agreed it was the most delicious meal they'd ever had; they also knew that they would probably never be able to afford its like again. As they walked home, Ann said a silent prayer of thanks to her father and John held her arm protectively, looking forward to introducing her to Jane.

* * * * *

At Mass next morning, John thanked God for his lovely new wife and prayed that Jane would be home with them soon. Ann had prepared her own room for Jane, putting a nice, bright cover on the bed and a small cabinet beside it for her clothes.

'I hope Jane will be happy here, John.'

'I know she will, and I'm grateful to you for all that you've done for her.' In the early afternoon, they set out for the Orphans' Home. John wore Auld Slowey's jacket that he'd worn for the wedding - he wanted to look more prosperous than he had on his previous visit.

'You look very smart, John - they'll surely be glad to release Jane to you, but I suppose we must be prepared for it to take a few days. They might want to visit us first, to make sure we have room for her.'

'That's possible, but hopefully it won't take long. The sooner she leaves, the sooner some other poor wean can have her place.'

They reached James Morrison Street. In front of the large, imposing door, John felt his stomach churn. He remembered all too well how he'd been treated the last time he'd come with James. *He must be strong and not let Ann see how nervous he was.* He reached up and raised the knocker, letting it strike the door. They heard footsteps, then a young woman opened the door.

'Yes, can ah help ye?'

'We'd like to see whoever's in charge, please. Is it Mr Galbraith?'

'I dinnae ken if he's in - ah'll check. Wait here.' She disappeared along the corridor, returning to say, 'He's oot the noo, but Miss Mathieson is coming to speak tae ye. Come intae the office.' She led them into the office that John remembered from the night he had first brought Jane here. A few minutes later, Miss Mathieson entered.

'Good afternoon. Can I ask your name and your business with Mr Galbraith?'

'I'm John Anderson and this is my wife, Ann. We've come to arrange for my sister Jane to come and live with us as we now have a room for her.'

'I see... Jane Anderson, you say? She's not been here for many months.'

'But where is she?'

'She went to our Orphan Homes Village at Bridge of Weir, last year if I remember correctly.'

'I wasn't told, but, if you'd kindly tell us how to get there, we'll go for her.'

'I'm afraid you can't; she's no longer there.' As John's face grew red with confusion, Miss Mathieson said, 'I think I hear Mr Galbraith arriving back. I'll see if he'll speak to you.' She quickly left the room and they could hear voices in the hall before Mr Galbraith came in.

'Mr Anderson, I'm told you're enquiring about Jane. You'll be glad to know that she's on her way to a wonderful new life.'

'A new life? I don't understand. I told you I would find a place for her to live with me.'

'And I told you that when you put her in the care of Quarrier's Homes, you signed her over to us. It's therefore our place, legally, to decide what is best for her. She sailed earlier this week to Canada with many other fortunate children previously in our care.' John staggered back, his face now ashen.

'To Canada - without a goodbye from her family? How is that possible? Did she want to go?'

'Jane knows that she's going to a better life than you can ever offer her. She'll be with a family who want her and will care for her in a beautiful country with lots of opportunity. You've not been her family for a long time now.'

'But you sent me away. I only wanted you to care for her until I could take her back.'

'Whatever you thought, the fact is that she's no longer here. Her new family has already been chosen; transfer papers have been signed and she will be with them soon.'

'Do you have an address where I can write to her?'

'We don't recommend contact once a child has emigrated. She must be given the chance to settle without distraction.' He explained that the Canadian organisers arranged placements and he didn't know her new address. He assured John that their inspectors would be checking regularly to make sure she was well and happy, and that Mr and Mrs Quarrier were kindly travelling with the children to ensure their comfort and safety on the journey. 'Go home, Mr Anderson, and don't worry about Jane. She's a very lucky girl. Now you must excuse me - Miss Mathieson will show you out.' He strode from the room and Miss Mathieson stood at the door to usher them out. She kept her eyes downcast and didn't look at the young couple. John had difficulty walking to the door. Ann took his arm till they were on the pavement outside.

'Oh, John, dear, I'm so sorry. I know how disappointed you must be.'

'I feel defeated, Ann, helpless. Surely what they've done is wrong.'

'It seems they have the law on their side.'

'I'll never see Jane again. I can't believe it. I told her I'd come back for her and I've missed her by only a few days. What must she be thinking?'

'Jane will know you love her, John, but maybe she is going to a better life than we could give her here.'

'I dearly hope so, but I'll never forgive myself for not seeing her before she went.'

'That wasn't your fault, John. They wouldn't let you. Surely if she hadn't wanted to go, she would have got a message to you.' John shook his head, bewildered. The joy of the previous day had vanished. He felt torn between sorrow at the loss of his sister and the knowledge that he had a new wife to look after. *Ann needed him to be strong and he would try.*

'Let's go home, Ann. I can't bear to be here any longer.' He took her hand and they headed back, oblivious to everything around them.

31

The storm continued to rage around the Nestorian. Mr and Mrs Quarrier stood at the door to Captain Henderson's cabin, buffeted by the wind. Mrs Quarrier wiped her eyes as her husband knocked on the door. The Captain opened it, saying, 'Come away in quickly. Be careful of the step.' He hurriedly leaned on the door to close it behind them. In the corner of his cabin, a small stove burned brightly and its warmth filled the cosy room. Wall lamps were reflected in the polished wood of the panelling and the highly-polished table in the centre. The Captain waved towards several leather chairs, indicating that they should sit down. 'I'm sorry we've had to meet tonight under such circumstances. I had already arranged to have you dine with me tomorrow, as you know, but the business in hand can't wait. Please join me in a glass of port - it may ease the burden on you of what I have to say.' He took some crystal glasses and a decanter of ruby-red port from a sideboard, and poured them each a glass. He held his up - 'Good health and better fortune.' They sipped from the glasses, enjoying the warmth of the liquid.

'Now we must discuss the dreadful accident which has happened. As you know, the child was killed instantly and that, at least, was a blessing in the circumstances. Her body's still in the infirmary room where I took her. I generally take the place of a doctor on board, but in this case there was nothing to be done. However, my First Mate confirmed that the girl was dead, and this has been entered in the ship's log: we now have to deal with the disposal of her body.

'Can this be done when we reach Canada?' asked Mrs Quarrier.

'I'm afraid not. Regulations don't permit me to carry a dead body on board for so long. She must be buried at sea and you, Mr Quarrier, as the person in charge of the party, must sign a letter giving me permission for this: it is our legal duty.' He took a letter from a drawer in the desk and placed it in front of Mr Quarrier.

'Does the child have family in Scotland or in Canada?'

'None at all, Captain Henderson.'

'In that case, the matter is simple. You have sole responsibility. Please sign here.' He pointed to the bottom of the letter and slid a feather pen and ink across the desk. Mr Quarrier read the content of the letter, dipped the feather quill in the ink and signed his name, sighing deeply. He took a drink of port and passed the paper back. Mrs Quarrier sipped quietly from her glass, holding a hand to her forehead.

'Thank you, Mr Quarrier. Now we must make arrangements. My First Mate advises that the storm will have gone by the morning. I propose we have the burial ceremony early, before other passengers come up on deck. It would not be pleasant, for the other children to see.'

'Agreed', replied Mr Quarrier.

'Please join me at the stern of the ship, behind my cabin, at 0700 hours. In the meantime, I'll prepare the child's body for burial unless you wish to assist, Mrs Quarrier.'

'Of course I will, Captain.'

'In that case, we'll have another port to fortify us beforehand.' He replenished all their glasses and they drank gratefully. They then made their way along the deck to the nearby cabin being used as the infirmary, holding tightly onto the rails. Captain Henderson held the door ajar to let them enter and closed it quickly behind them. Inside the small cabin, an oil lamp cast an eerie glow. There were two bunks with a cabinet between them. Tilly's body lay on one bunk, covered with a sheet; at her feet was a folded piece of canvas. Captain Henderson pulled back the sheet to reveal Tilly's face, which was white as marble but streaked with blood from a gaping wound in her head.
Mrs Quarrier shuddered and put her hand over her mouth. Mr Quarrier put his arm around her.

'I'm sorry, my dear, that you're having to deal with this.'

'It's the least I can do for the poor child.'

'I'm much obliged to you, given that she's a young girl.' The Captain opened out the canvas sheet and laid it on the other bunk, saying, 'If you could wash her then put her in this, I'd be very grateful. I'll come back later and stitch the ends.' He pointed to the cabinet on which there was a ewer of water, a basin, some cloths, a large, curved needle and a bobbin of twine. The two men left the cabin and Mrs Quarrier set to work, cleaning Tilly then wrapping her in the canvas sheet. Task over, she made her way back to her cabin, trying to forget the sight of Tilly's poor body.

At 7 o'clock the next morning, Mr and Mrs Quarrier met Captain Henderson and his officers at the stern, as arranged. The ship was no longer rolling from side to side, but a chill mist hung in the air. Two crewmen arrived carrying a wooden board between them: on it was Tilly's body, wrapped in the canvas shroud. They stood in the middle of the group; Captain Henderson took out his bible and read aloud a prayer for the dead, then together they recited the Lord's Prayer. Finally, the Captain said, 'And now, dear Lord, we commit her body to the deep.' The two crewmen stepped forward and laid the board on the rail of the ship. They gently tipped it up and Tilly's body slid slowly over the side and into the sea. It disappeared immediately under the waves as the ship moved forward. Mrs Quarrier caught her breath and turned away. 'I thank you all for your assistance in this tragic affair', said the Captain, 'but I must now leave you, in order to carry on with my other duties. Good day.' As he left and the group dispersed, Mr Quarrier patted his wife's back. 'Go back to our cabin, my dear, and I'll have your breakfast brought to you. I know what an ordeal this has been for you.'

32

'Wake up, children; rise and have some breakfast. The weather's better today.' As Miss Sliman passed, Jane called to her,

'Miss Sliman, is Tilly still in the infirmary?'

'I haven't heard anything about her this morning, Jane, but don't worry. You'll be going up on deck soon and you can find out then how she is. Try to eat just now.' The usual breakfast of porridge and dry bread was brought to the sleeping quarters with some tea. The ship seemed to have stopped rolling and Jane managed a little of everything. Lizzie and Mary still looked pale from the previous day's sickness, but each ate some food. They all waited anxiously to see if it would come back up. They felt a little queasy but the food stayed in their stomachs. Miss Sliman passed through again, calling, 'Up onto the top deck now, please, and have a walk. I'm sure you'll be glad of it.'

The girls made their way up. The mist had cleared and the sun was out but it was still bitterly cold. Dozens of boys and girls moved around, seeking fresh air for the first time in what seemed like many days. Most were walking very carefully - pale and shaky on their feet. Some were clinging onto the ship's rail and looking down into the waves beneath. Nothing was visible but the grey sea all around. Jane shivered at the sight of it and looked instead at the cabins along the centre of the deck. 'I wonder which one Tilly's in.' A sailor was working with some ropes nearby and Jane asked him, 'Where's the infirmary cabin, please?' He pointed at a cabin near the Captain's. When they reached the cabin the sailor had pointed to, they saw it had several round windows but they were too high to see through. Jane knocked warily on the door. When there was no reply, she put her hand out to open the door. Just then an officer approached.

'What are you doing there?'

'Our friend Tilly's in there. We'd like to see her, please.'

'I think you're mistaken. As far as I know there are no patients at the moment. In any case, you would need permission from the Captain even if your friend was there.' He tried the door handle, but it would not move. 'No, girls, it's locked right enough. On your way now.' They moved away immediately.

'Maybe she's feeling better and is with Mrs Quarrier now,' said Lizzie.

'Prob'ly' said Mary. Jane couldn't help feeling anxious, but realised they could do nothing more till they saw one of the Quarriers. They continued with their walk, chatting with others on the way, glad to see familiar faces; some who knew her asked about Tilly and how she was. 'We don't know,' said Jane, shrugging her shoulders.

When the midday bell rang, they walked towards the staircase, but Miss Sliman was waiting there. 'We're meeting in the chapel before we eat. Continue in this direction and you will see Miss Quarrier waiting at the chapel door.' She spoke seriously without her usual ready smile. They found Miss Quarrier at the door of a large cabin and, looking very serious, she ushered them through the doorway. Jane stopped to ask about Tilly, but Miss Quarrier raised her hand and shook her head. 'Please just go in, Jane. My father is going to speak to you all.' Inside, there were rows of wooden benches facing a long wooden table and behind the table was a cross on the wall; beside it a lectern with a bible. Mr Quarrier stood behind it, looking very stern. As the children came in, they fell silent and sat on the benches, crushing together to let everyone in. Eventually, Miss Sliman and Miss Quarrier entered, nodded to Mr Quarrier and closed the door. They stood with heads bowed.

Mr Quarrier coughed nervously, then began, 'Good afternoon, children. Welcome to the ship's chapel. We will have our Sunday service here tomorrow, but I must speak to you this morning before rumours start to go round. Some of you already know that there was an accident in one of the sleeping quarters yesterday when young Tilly was badly hurt. I have to tell you that our good Captain Henderson did his best for her but was unable to save her. We've lost Tilly but she's now safe in the arms of Jesus where she can never be harmed again. We must accept that this is our dear Lord's plan. When he calls, we must go to him. We will now pray for Tilly's eternal soul. Please bow your heads.' As he began the Lord's Prayer and everyone else joined in, Mary grasped Jane's arm. 'Does that mean Tilly's dead?' Her eyes were wide with terror. Jane nodded and could not hold in a sob. On her other side, Lizzie was speechless, shaking her head in disbelief. As if from a distance, they could hear Mr Quarrier say, 'May she rest in peace.' then heard him telling them to go now and eat, and the children filed out in silence. Jane was barely aware of walking along the deck. In the dining area, other children began to eat, but Jane felt she would never eat again. She sat with her eyes closed and, in her mind, saw Tilly disappearing under the falling bunk. As soon as she could, she went back to the sleeping quarters and climbed into Tilly's bunk. Her tears flowed then for her little friend who could have been safe in Bridge of Weir but had begged to go with them. If this was God's plan, it was a cruel one.

33

The days passed in a blur. Fog, wind or rain kept the children below deck in their bunks: they hardly knew if it was day or night. Food arrived to tempt them to eat – herrings, ship's biscuits, oranges – but these were often left untouched: many of them were still suffering from sea sickness. When the weather was clearer, they would walk around on the top deck watching the busy sailors at their work. The men always seemed to be scrubbing decks and polishing the brass frames around the portholes of the cabins. Some of the crew set up swings made from rope, with canvas for seats, and hung them from beams below deck, so that the children could have some amusement. This was fine on still days, but if the boat was rolling they were difficult to control. Sometimes, the children were called to look overboard at giant fish swimming along beside the ship. Always, they were encouraged to read the bibles which each of them had been given as gifts from Quarrier supporters in Scotland, but Jane found little comfort in hers. Time and again, she woke up in the night imagining she could feel Tilly's hand slipping from hers as she fell under the heavy bunk which killed her. She wished they were back again in Bridge of Weir in the sunshine, but could hardly imagine ever being on dry land again.

It was a cold, foggy afternoon when Mr Quarrier came to say Grace and then asked them,

'Does anyone know why today, the twenty-fourth of May, is a special day?'

'Are we nearly in Canada?' asked one boy.

'Not for a few more days yet. No, today is the sixtieth birthday of our dear Queen Victoria. To celebrate this, the cook has made a special dinner of salt beef and vegetables and this will be followed by tea-cakes for you. This evening we will meet here after tea for some singing and recitation. If you have a song to sing or a poem to recite, then practise it this afternoon. Now enjoy your special meal.' As he turned to leave, one of the older girls asked,

'Please, Sir, is there a king or queen in Canada?'

'Why, our own dear Victoria is Queen of Canada too, as it is part of the British Empire. This will be another reason for you to feel at home there.' The food was then brought in; the salt beef was not to everyone's taste, but the vegetables made a pleasant change and the tea-cakes a welcome treat.

In the afternoon, the children were taken in groups to learn the first verse of what they were told was called the National Anthem, 'God Save The Queen'. Most of the children had never heard it before but quickly learned it, enjoying the novelty of singing something different. As the fog continued, they went below and continued to practise, to break the monotony. The girls could hear the boys further along the deck singing the same words but in a more rousing fashion, accompanied by the stamping of feet. They had all been told to wash and be tidy for the evening concert, so the girls took turns in the toilet area and helped brush each other's hair; there was indeed an air of excitement - some were even smiling.

At tea-time, on a wooden stand beside Mr Quarrier was a picture of a stern-looking woman all dressed in black. 'Silence now, children,' he called and a hush fell over the room. 'Here we have a picture of Queen Victoria whose birthday we are celebrating today. You can see that she is still in mourning clothes for her beloved Prince Albert, who was taken from her many years ago, but all across the Empire, people like us will be giving thanks that such a great queen is still with us. She has many children whom she loves and some of them live in other countries, so I have no doubt that she would wish you all the best lives you can make for yourselves with your new families. Let us sing the National Anthem in praise of her. Please stand.' The children stood up and Miss Quarrier stepped forward to lead them. When the last notes faded, Mr Quarrier called out,

'Three cheers for Queen Victoria. Hip, hip...' Three times, the rest of the party answered,

'Hooray.'

'Well done, children. I'm proud of you. Now sit and enjoy your food.' Trays of fruit and biscuits were brought to the tables and everyone ate heartily. Children sang and others recited poems they had learned; the last song of the evening was from a little boy who sang *Wee*

Willie Winkie. At the last words 'Are all the children in their beds? It's past 8 o'clock', he bowed low and everyone clapped their hands, laughing. 'On that note,' called Mr Quarrier, 'we should retire to bed. God bless you all, children. Sleep well.' As she settled down to sleep, Jane thought of the old queen dressed in black, '*So even queens lose people and are sad.*'

34

Sunday passed quietly, with the usual Sabbath service in the ship's chapel in the morning. Fog continued to envelop the ship after dinner and the children went to their sleeping quarters where Miss Sliman read them some stories to pass the time. In the evening, they returned to the chapel for gospel-reading and hymn-singing, before retiring for the night. Sailors with lamps that gleamed eerily through the darkness stood on the deck to light their way, but they held onto each other for security.

Next day, the fog cleared in the afternoon and they were able to walk around the deck; it was bitterly cold. The sailors gave the girls lengths of fine rope with which to play at skipping, and this certainly helped warm them up. However, looking around them there was still nothing to see but ocean.

'D'ye think we'll ever get to Canada?' asked Lizzie.

'Ah don't care', said Mary, 'Ah jist want aff this boat anywhere.' Jane laughed.

'Not anywhere - somewhere with houses and people. That's what I miss.' They reminisced about Bridge of Weir and how good it had been, especially in the summer. None of them talked about their lives before the Orphan Homes; that was too painful now, and the misery of being on the ship was enough to cope with. The girls tried to skip with their ropes on deck the next day but it was covered in snow so instead they went below and played on the makeshift swings. At dinner, Mr Quarrier announced that they had reached the Gulf of St Lawrence. 'This means that our long journey is almost over. We just have to be patient with the weather - the Captain has assured me it will clear soon.'

When Wednesday dawned brightly and stayed dry, they managed to play on deck all afternoon, then they were told to organise their trunks for arriving in Canada. They could hardly believe it – they would finally be landing in Quebec next day. 'Don't forget to pack your bibles.' They hurriedly checked their trunks, and sat them on the floor beside their bunks. They chattered excitedly.

'D'ye think we'll meet our new families tomorrow?' Lizzie asked.

'Don't know; I think we have to go to that Miss Bilbrough's house first, at least that's what Miss Sliman told me', said Mary. Jane hardly slept that night and in the morning was exhausted. However, she noticed with relief that the engine was no longer making a noise and the ship was no longer rolling. Miss Sliman arrived with breakfast and told them they had indeed arrived in Quebec. 'You must stay below deck here till you're called, then we'll leave the ship, but we still have a long journey by rail and road ahead of us. Up till now your behaviour has been wonderful, children, and that must continue, so just do exactly as you're told, please. Eat up now - you'll need all your strength for the days ahead.'

Sailors came and took their trunks for unloading. Soon the children were called to the top deck in groups. The sun was shining in a bright blue sky. They could see the bustling dock where newly-disembarked passengers from several ships hurried along pushing trolleys of luggage, and dock-workers loaded goods onto decks, then lowered them into holds. The noise and the sights reminded Jane of Broomielaw, and of James - she wondered where he was now. She'd been young when he left, but every time they passed Broomielaw afterwards, her mother would say, 'Our James could be on a ship like that – please God he's safe.' Ropes had been tied to several capstans on the dockside and a gangplank put in place from the S.S. Nestorian. An officer stood at the top holding a sheaf of papers. As each child passed him, he asked his or her name and ticked it off on a list. Another officer helped the smaller children onto the gangplank, telling them to hold tightly onto the ropes at its side for balance.

As they came off onto the dockside, a Canadian immigration official asked their names again, to tick off on his list, then they were sent to stand in two lines in front of a huge shed, boys on one side and girls on the other - as usual, Jane, Lizzie and Mary kept together. Inside the shed, they could see large wooden cubicles with curtains and wondered what was about to happen. Miss Sliman and Miss Quarrier arrived, repeating as they walked along beside the lines of nervous boys and girls, 'Don't worry, children. This is all part of the immigration process. Inside the shed, doctors will examine you and check that you're quite fit to enter Canada before we can leave the dock. Wait here till you're called inside. When you've been checked, you'll leave by a door at the back of the shed where we'll meet you.' Lizzie looked at the others, wide-eyed,

'What if we're not fit? D'ye think we'll have to go back on the boat?'

'I hope not', said Mary; Jane stayed silent, thoughtful. The line slowly diminished as, one by one, the children were called inside: they couldn't see anyone leaving, which added to the mystery.

Eventually, Jane was called into the shed and directed by a woman in uniform into one of the cubicles. Coming in from the sunlight, the shed seemed gloomy and stuffy and it also felt strange not to feel the ship moving beneath her feet. Jane stumbled a little but managed to keep her balance. The woman pulled a curtain aside, and inside the cubicle was a table; a tall-looking man with thick, dark hair sat behind it and looked at her over the rim of his glasses. She heard the curtain swish back in place behind her.

'Name, please?'

'Jane Anderson, Sir.'

'Well, at least they taught you some manners. Where you from?'

'Glasgow, Sir.'

'Right, let's see if you're fit and well - it's probably too much to expect for you to be clean as well, after your long sea journey.' Jane's face reddened.

'We did get washed, Sir, but we couldn't have a bath.'

'I hope that wasn't a complaint, girl. You should be grateful to be here at all.' Jane was lost for words to reply; looked down at the wooden floor instead.

'Take off your pinafore, petticoat and shoes - leave them on the bench over there then come back to me. And be quick about it; I've got plenty more of you lot to check over.' Jane undressed quickly and went back to stand in front of the table. 'Round this side, where I can see you properly.' She moved awkwardly around the table, trying to avoid touching it with her body. The doctor sighed and checked his watch. He stood up then and loomed over Jane. He tilted her head back and looked into her eyes, into her mouth and into her ears. She was asked to read letters from a chart on the wall. He put a trumpet-shaped metal instrument against her chest and listened at its narrow end, repeating this on her back. A weighing machine with figures on it was pointed to.

'Stand on there. Do you know what age you are?'

'Eight and a few months, Sir.' She'd been trying to work this out recently and was glad she could speak confidently. He noted her height and weight.

'You seem a little small, but that's fairly usual, I guess. Walk to the end of the cubicle and back, then bend to touch your toes.' Jane did as she was asked, struggling a little to reach her toes but determined not to give this man any reason to criticise her. He then felt her tummy and asked about her toilet habits. She dearly wished this ordeal to be over, whatever the result. At last he said, 'Right, put your clothes back on.' When she was dressed, he pulled back the curtain and pointed to a large door at the end of the shed.

'Through there and re-join your group. Welcome to Canada.'

35

Jane emerged from the immigration shed to join the line of girls who'd been examined before her; the boys were in a separate line. 'Over here, Jane,' shouted Mary and Lizzie, and she ran to join them. Miss Sliman stood nearby with an older man the children didn't recognise. The warmth of the sun was so enjoyable: they smiled at each other, beginning to feel their balance return. Looking around, they could see a railway station beyond the landward entrance to the dock. A train steamed past with a clanging of bells and the blast of a horn. Jumping a little, the girls let out a small scream and then laughed quietly together. In every other direction were fields of various colours - only the occasional house could be seen in the distance. The long lines of children grew till they were all out. By now, faces were red and girls were using their hats to fan themselves. 'Girls, listen please', called Miss Sliman. 'This is Mr Rae from the shipping company. He'll take us to the railway station for the next part of our journey. Stay in line and walk smartly.' They could see Mr Quarrier speaking to the boys; then they all set off.

A horse and cart passed them, loaded with trunks. It had unloaded them and was returning towards the docks before they reached the station. There, a train was waiting and the trunks were being loaded onto the last carriage. Mr Quarrier climbed onto the steps of a carriage to address them. 'You'll be brought on board in a few minutes and we'll be on this train until tomorrow; however, we have very comfortable carriages with toilet facilities, and food will be served to you shortly.' Mary clasped her hands and rolled her eyes, saying 'Good. My feet are sore: I'll be glad to sit anywhere.' He stepped down to speak to Mr Rae, shaking his hand, and Miss Sliman led the girls onto the train; the boys were led onto carriages further down the train.

Inside, the train was stuffy, but the long seats were comfortable and there were racks above their heads to store their capes and hats. Long boards fixed to the sides of the train served as tables where the girls sat down gratefully and Miss Sliman opened some windows. The train's whistle sounded, bells were rung and the train slowly steamed out of the station. Outside, there were fields as far as the eye could see;

in the sunlight they seemed to glow golden. The train gradually built up speed till the fields passed by in a blur. Bread and fruit and water were served. Jane was glad of it as she was hungry and the water cooled her down, though the movement of the train made her feel as if she was back on the ship. *How weary she was of this long journey.*

All through the afternoon, the girls looked out of the windows, hoping to catch sight of people and houses, but all they saw were fields and animals. Cows close to the railway line turned their large heads as the train passed. 'I wish we could slow down and see them better,' said Mary. Eventually, boredom and fatigue set in, and girls fell asleep where they sat, heads lolling to the train's rhythm. At tea-time, they were wakened, and bread and soup were brought which revived them. When darkness fell, many hours were spent wondering and chatting about their future and wishing they could find out about their new families. When Miss Sliman passed to check on them, Lizzie said,

'Miss, when will we know who our new families are? Will they be waiting for us when we get off the train?'

'You must be patient, Lizzie. Our friends at Belleville are organising your placements. We'll reach there tomorrow afternoon and we may know more then.' Towards 10 o'clock, the train began to slow down. A conductor came along the corridor, calling, 'Approaching Montreal for a one-hour stop.' The children stood up to put on their capes and bonnets: it was only then they realised how stiff they were. 'Oh, my legs are so sore,' said Jane. They hobbled around, trying to get the feeling back in their limbs. They eagerly looked out when the train pulled into the station but could only see the station building beside the platform. There were lights inside; all around it was dark. They were led inside and given a small supper in the half-light before going back onto the train.

They settled down for the night, but, with little room to spare, they had to remain seated. Some laid their heads on each other's shoulders but there was little comfort to be found with the movement of the train. Others rested their heads on the tables with folded capes beneath them. Few slept properly throughout the long night. In the morning they presented an untidy picture, with hair tousled or matted with sweat, and clothes crumpled. Many of them were close to tears, their eyes sticky with sleep. They took turns at squeezing past the others to go to the toilet cubicles which by now smelt horrible. When breakfast was served, they could barely eat. The next few hours were spent looking out of the window where were still lots of fields to be seen, some with tall grasses; some with cows or horses. Occasionally, low houses flashed past but they were too far away for them to be able to see people around them. The sky remained bright blue, and sunshine sparkled prettily on ponds they passed near the railway line. Again and again, the windows were opened to let in fresh air which was very welcome.

In the early afternoon, the train began to slow and the conductor called out, 'Approaching Belleville now - make sure you take all your belongings with you before alighting. Mind the steps as you go.' There was a welcome flurry of activity as they got off the train and arranged themselves in lines again, glad to be nearing the end of their journey. They recognised Miss Bilbrough standing on the platform, dressed in a bright cotton dress and straw hat. She shook hands with the Quarriers and Miss Sliman.

'Welcome to Belleville, dear friends. I trust your journey was suitably comfortable.'

'It was indeed, Miss Bilbrough. Now we're looking forward to seeing Marchmont.'

'I have carriages waiting for you, and the porters will load your trunks. We'll be in Marchmont within the hour.' Once again, children and luggage were loaded onto carts. Horses tossed their heads and shook their tails, trying to dislodge troublesome flies. Miss Bilbrough, the Quarriers and Miss Sliman climbed into the front carriage and, at a shout from their driver, the group set off.

36

The convoy of open carriages trundled along, the children on the wooden benches bouncing back and forth as the wheels rolled over the rough ground. Despite their tiredness, they looked around them curiously at this unfamiliar country where their new lives would soon begin. Trees lined the route, tall trees of every shade of green, and beautiful flowers. Jane thought back to the journey from Bridge of Weir to Quarrier's Village, also by carriage but in the cold and driving rain. Here, the warm sun shone on them and made shifting patterns on the road as it filtered through the trees. From time to time, they passed wooden houses set back from the road. Some had verandas outside where dogs lay sleeping. The more energetic of the animals ran to the roadside to bark at the passing vehicles, but soon ran back to the shade of their verandas, panting with their efforts. At one point, they saw a huge expanse of water through the trees and the carriages slowed to a halt. In the front carriage, the adults stood and looked out over the water, shielding their eyes from the sun with their hands.

'We're not goin' on another boat, are we?' moaned Mary. Their driver turned, laughing.

'Not today, child. That's our beautiful Lake Ontario - one of the five Great Lakes. Get a good look while you have the chance; it's a sight to behold.' It did indeed look lovely in the sunlight, stretching out into the distance.

After a few minutes, the convoy moved off again. Soon, it left the road and began to climb a long gravel driveway. Up ahead, they could see a huge house, built of brick and with dozens of windows, each with wooden shutters opened against the walls. Several large chimneys topped the roof of the three-storey building. Around the ground floor stretched a long veranda with its own roof held up by pillars. The whole scene was bathed in sunlight and the children looked up at the house, wide-eyed, and smiled at each other. The carriages carrying the girls came to a halt in front of the house, while those carrying the boys went on round the back and out of sight.

Miss Sliman came and called, 'We've arrived, girls, so climb down and line up, ready to go in.' They could see their trunks being unloaded and laid out on the veranda. They were sent forward, a few at a time, to find their trunks and arrange themselves beside two large wooden doors. They were led into a large hall with wooden floors and a staircase winding up to an upper floor. Miss Bilbrough stood at the bottom of the staircase. 'Welcome to Marchmont. I'll show you to your dormitory where you can leave your trunks.' They followed her upstairs and into a long dormitory with iron-framed beds along two sides. The windows stood open and the sun made pools of light on the floor. They could see Lake Ontario; Jane thought it looked beautiful and was happy to keep looking out. 'Take a bed each, put your trunk beside it with your capes and bonnets on top then come downstairs to eat.' Their boots clicked on the floorboards as they moved to choose their beds; Jane, Lizzie and Mary smiled at finding beds close to one another.

Downstairs, they were led into a big dining-room and Jane was suddenly conscious of hunger pangs - her mouth watered at the delicious aroma of the food to come. When they were all settled, Miss Bilbrough said Grace. Several young women came and served their food - chicken legs and steaming potatoes with bright orange carrots were piled on their plates, followed by dishes of apple pie and cream. They ate heartily - Canada was seeming better by the minute.

After tea, they were taken to bathrooms on the upper floor, where they bathed and had their hair washed and doused with vinegar. They were given clean cotton nightdresses and their clothes were taken for washing. 'Right, girls, upstairs with you.' shouted one of the young women, - 'straight to bed and you'll get your clothes back tomorrow.' In the dormitory, the windows and shutters were closed and oil-lamps had been lit and hung around the walls; Jane wished she could look out over the lake again and see what it looked like in the moonlight. Miss Sliman came to say goodnight; 'Sleep well, girls; we've a busy day ahead of us tomorrow - and don't forget to say your prayers.' As she left the room, Lizzie whispered, 'I don't think I can sleep. I wish we could stay here forever.' A short time later, they were all fast asleep.

Meanwhile, the Quarriers and Miss Sliman were meeting with Miss Bilbrough.

'We must thank you for that delicious meal, Miss Bilbrough. It has quite revived us and I know the children appreciated it too. I'm sure that after a good rest tonight, they'll be fit to travel on.'

'You're welcome - glad you enjoyed it. Many of them will be travelling tomorrow, particularly those going on by train. I've arranged homes for about one hundred of the children already and we've tried as far as possible to match them to the families' requirements. A number of them will be picked up directly from here - their new families, whose references have already been checked, will collect them throughout the coming week. Those making journeys of within two or three hours by train will travel in the care of our reliable train conductors. Their families have been alerted to their arrival times at local stations and will meet them there. In a few days' time, Mr and Mrs Quarrier, you'll travel with the boys going further afield; Miss Quarrier and Miss Sliman will travel with the girls in that situation.' The group nodded enthusiastically.

'And what of those remaining? Do you expect them to find homes soon?' asked Mr Quarrier.

'Certainly. We've already had applications from many families who want them and we're merely awaiting the relevant references from their church ministers. This is something that we absolutely insist upon. It means that, as well as knowing the families are of good character, we can be more secure in the knowledge that the children will be sent to church as well as school. As you know, they attend school as the seasonal work requirements of their host farms will allow, but generally they attend church or Sunday school each week. I fully expect that, within the week, they'll all be suitably placed.'

'What marvellous work you've done on our behalf, Miss Bilbrough. You're to be admired for your diligence.'

'My pleasure, Mrs Quarrier. The reward is seeing how the lives of these poor children are improved.' She explained how inspectors visited the children as often as possible to check on their welfare, and that if a placing had not been successful, children would be sent back to her to be re-homed. 'It's rarely necessary,' she added.

'That's all very satisfactory, and it's wonderful to see Marchmont for ourselves. It's certainly an asset to our organisation in Scotland.'

'Well, my dears,' Mr Quarrier interrupted, 'I think we've kept Miss Bilbrough from bed long enough. I suggest we all retire for a well-deserved rest.'

* * * * *

The children were wakened by Miss Sliman opening the windows and shutters. Sunlight streamed in and it took Jane a moment to remember where she was. 'Good morning, girls; time to get up. Use the toilet cubicles and wash yourselves in the bathrooms along the corridor. Breakfast will be served in the dining-room. Keep on your nightdresses for the moment - your clean clothes will be given out after breakfast, so waste no time, please - we have much to do.' Obedient as ever, the girls followed their instructions and soon were seated at the dining-room table, where enormous breakfasts were served. Eating at a table which did not vibrate with the movement of a ship or a train was a relief. The hour after breakfast was spent getting back their clean clothes from the laundry, putting some on and packing the others in their trunk - packing away her cape made Jane feel strange because it felt connected to Quarrier's. That done, they were then allowed out into the large garden surrounding the Home to take advantage of the warm, fresh air. Jane, Lizzie and Mary sat on the grass, turning their faces up to the sun and enjoying the quietness around them.

'I wonder when we'll find out about our new families,' said Mary.

'I don't care,' Lizzie replied, 'I'm happy to stay here.' Just then, Miss Sliman arrived with a list in her hand.

'Jane, could you go upstairs and bring down your trunk, please? Put it out on the veranda and stay beside it.'

'What about us, Miss?' asked Mary.

'It's not your turn yet, but it will be soon. Don't worry.' She went on round the garden, selecting girls from her list to fetch their trunks. Jane looked a little anxiously at her friends and turned to go.

'Hurry up and come back,' said Lizzie, 'and we'll make daisy chains.'

Standing on the porch with her trunk, Jane was joined by other girls with theirs. Miss Sliman then returned with an armful of cardboard squares on strings.

'Well done, girls. Now you are about to start a new adventure. You'll go by carriage back to Belleville Station – you can see the carriages are just arriving. I'll accompany you there, then you'll all go by train to meet your new families. You'll each wear a little sign with your name and destination on it so that the conductor will know where you are getting off.'

'Are you not coming with us, Miss Sliman?'

'Not on the train, my dear - I have to come back and get everyone else ready to leave.' Two carriages stopped in front of the house and while the other two continued round the building to where the boys were, their drivers began loading the trunks, shouting, 'Right girls, climb aboard.' Jane suddenly felt panicked.

'Can I go and tell my friends that I'm going, Miss?'

'Sorry, Jane, there's no time. You've a train to catch.' They all climbed on and the carriages set off immediately. As they made their way back to Belleville, a wagon approached from the opposite direction and the driver called to theirs, waving him to stop.

'Are these Home Children? Where are they going?'

'The railway station to catch a train.'

'Are there any left? I was hoping to pick one today.'

'Plenty there for the picking, I should think,' laughed their driver and they set off again.

The road to the station seemed shorter than their journey the previous day; in no time at all, they'd arrived and Miss Sliman went round, placing the small cardboard signs around their necks. On Jane's it said 'Jane Anderson' on one side: 'Pickering Post Office, Ontario – E. O'Brien' on the other. *What can that mean?* she wondered. She could see Mr Quarrier further along the platform, hanging signs around the boys' necks. When the train chugged into the station and stopped, a man in uniform stepped down. The boys and girls were put in separate carriages and their trunks were loaded on with them. Miss Sliman and Mr Quarrier, came forward to wave them off. 'Goodbye and good luck, all of you. Put the training you have had from us to good use and make us proud of you. God bless.' Mr Quarrier waved his hat in the air. The girls looked at each other. Some of the younger ones were quietly sniffling. Jane felt close to tears but tried taking deep breaths and blinking. The conductor came round, checking the destinations on their signs. 'Don't get outta your seats, mind; I'll be checking on you.' Within moments the train had left the station and once again Jane faced the unknown.

37

The train was heading in the opposite direction from Quebec, but the scenery was unchanging. Field after field of green, and sometimes golden, grass on one side and the huge Lake Ontario on the other, sparkling in the sunlight; Jane thought how pretty it looked. *But where were all the people? Sometimes they passed wooden houses like the ones they'd seen near Belleville, but there must be others. Surely, they couldn't hold all the people who lived here. In the tenements of Glasgow, it was hard to walk for a few minutes without meeting dozens of inhabitants... maybe Pickering would be busier.*

At various stations along the line, children were set down on platforms. Sometimes, people came forward to meet them, usually middle-aged men in work clothes, boots and hats; sometimes the children were left alone on the platforms with their trunks, watching the train disappearing into the distance. Jane hoped someone would meet her. *If no-one came, what would she do? Try to get on the next train back? Then what?* She shivered at the thought. Looking around the compartment, she thought everyone looked as nervous as she was; there had been a little conversation to start with, but everyone was quiet now.

A burly, scruffy man passing along the corridor turned back and opened the compartment door. 'Well, what we got here? You girls dressed for a party? You sure are quiet.' His slow, drawling voice was loud and the conductor immediately appeared at his side.

'Can I help you, Sir?'

'Just wondering where these girls are headed in their fine clothes.'

'They're Home Children from Scotland on their way to new families. They're in my care for now.'

'Well, I'll be... They seem quiet - prob'ly dreamin' up some thievin' or other from what I hear.'

'They're doing no harm here, Sir. Please just go back to your own compartment an' leave them be.' With a last look round at the girls, the man moved on, smirking. The conductor put his head round the door, saying, 'Not long now - just a few more stops to make.' A few minutes later, she heard him call out, 'Approaching Pickering now. Make sure you take your belongings with you and mind the steps as you get off.' Jane was up on her feet and lifting her trunk when the conductor came for her. She looked around at the remaining girls. 'Cheerio,' she said and the others mumbled their goodbyes.

The train slowed and came to a halt, and the conductor took her trunk and placed it on the platform as Jane stepped down. There was no-one else in sight and she felt cold with dread. 'You'll find the Post Office round the back of the station,' said the conductor, pointing to a wooden gate. He stepped back on the train, the whistle sounded and the train went on its way. Jane lifted her trunk, but just as she reached the gate, a woman came through it. 'Are you Jane Anderson from the Glasgow Home?' Jane nodded her head but couldn't speak; her mouth felt suddenly dry. 'Well I'm Mrs O'Brien, so come right this way.' She didn't sound unpleasant and her accent was easy to understand, but she wasn't smiling. Jane walked along beside her, trying to look at her without being noticed. She seemed quite old. She wore a straw hat, but when she took it off to fan her face Jane could see her grey hair tied up on top of her head. Her brown arms were bare and she wore a faded cotton dress and sturdy boots. They walked past a wooden shed with a sign - 'Post Office' - above the door. Just beyond it, a horse with a cart attached was tied to a wooden fence, the horse tossing its head and snorting as Mrs O'Brien approached. 'Right. Let's get your luggage in the wagon and get on our way.' The woman took the trunk and swung it easily into the back of the wagon beside some sacks. When she took Jane's hand to help her up onto the long bench in front, her skin felt rough and lumpy but warm. She untied the horse's reins from the post and climbed in beside Jane. She shook the reins and clicked her tongue, and the horse moved off.

As they moved along, barely faster than a walking pace, Jane saw other buildings with shop signs: a grain store and a hardware shop and a few small houses. Wagons were tied to fences or posts, and dogs wandered around or lay in the shade on verandas. Mrs O'Brien waved to some women standing outside the grain store and they called out, 'Good day, Betty.'

'Who you got there?' asked one.

'This is our new addition from Scotland, come to live with us.'

'She's a lucky girl', said the other, 'I hope she knows it.'

'This is the township of Pickering, Jane - our farm is a bit further out; won't be long till we're there, though.' Jane nodded, still silent with apprehension. They passed a small church on the outskirts of the township, then went on out into the countryside where the wagon bumped and rattled over a rough track. The horse walked on as if it knew the way but it looked as if there was no other way to go - no tracks led off from the one they were on. It was hot, but the dappled sunlight through the trees was cooled by the motion of the wagon, and Jane was pleased to be outside and not on a stuffy train. Mrs O'Brien seemed to be concentrating on encouraging the horse with clicks of her teeth and small sounds, but made no more conversation.

After an hour or so, Jane could see a stone house up ahead with a gravel path leading to it. The horse quickened its pace as if anxious to get there now. As they approached, a young man in dungarees and boots came round the side of the house and came forward to grab the horse's bridle. Beside him trotted a big, black and white, long-haired dog, wagging its tail. Mrs O'Brien threw the young man the reins and climbed down.

'This is my son, Jimmy. Jimmy, this here's Jane.' He nodded to Jane and smiled.

'Hello, Jane.' His accent was a little different from his mother's, more like the train conductor's.

'Give Jane down her trunk and take the flour and sugar I got at the grain store into the pantry.' Mrs O'Brien helped Jane down from the bench and Jimmy handed her the trunk, then lifted the sacks from the wagon and strode ahead into the house; Jane followed with Mrs O'Brien. Going from the sunlight into the house, the interior was dark and Jane peered at her surroundings. She could see a stone floor, a big table and some chairs; at the back of the room a range with hooks and cooking pots hanging above it; a big dresser stood at the side wall. 'This here's the kitchen,' said Mrs O'Brien then led the way to a room off the kitchen at the back of the house, the dog circling round her till she patted its head. 'This is Jake. He barks a lot but he isn't mean, and he'll get to know you soon enough. We'll put your stuff here in the washhouse for now and see how we go. You'll be working in here a lot of the time anyway: it's where the laundry gets done and the well for water's just across the yard.' Several barrels and tubs stood on the stone floor against the far wall. There was a big enamel bath on a stand, with a tray underneath it holding the old embers. A low bed stood in the corner, covered with a patchwork quilt, beside it a small table with a jug and basin on top. Washing lines were draped across the room but nothing hung on them at the moment. Through a small window, Jane could see out into fields, behind some outbuildings where Jimmy was unhitching the wagon – he led the horse into one. There was also a door from the washhouse leading outside. 'Out there's the back yard. In summer we can hang the washing outside to dry; in winter we hang it in here - if you're not hanging out washing, keep the door closed. It'll keep you cool when the weather's hot and warm when it's cold.' She pointed to the jug and basin. 'Get freshened up and come through to the kitchen to eat.' Jane washed her face and hands in the cold water from the jug. After the first shock of the cold against her skin, she felt refreshed.

Back in the kitchen, she watched Mrs O'Brien slicing ham from a huge joint. She put some slices on a plate and added some vegetables from a dish on the dresser. Beside it she sat a big mug of milk. 'Set yourself down at the table, Jane. These are some leftovers from dinner. We'll have tea when the boys come in from the fields.' Jimmy put his head round the door.

'That's everything put away, Mother. I'll go back to the fields.'

'Tell Robbie Jane's here and he'll meet her at tea-time.'

'Right. He waved at Jane as he left and she waved back. As Jane ate, Mrs O'Brien said,

'I've got two good boys, Jane; just as well - I've no man now. My husband died of consumption a few years back. We manage fine, but I'm getting too tired now to cope with all the kitchen and laundry work, so I hope you'll be a good help to me. We came here from Scotland with six children, but I lost two girls to scarlet fever and two boys to diphtheria. Robbie and Jimmy have grown up here fine. Robbie's twenty-four and Jimmy's eighteen - they're really Canadians now. When the minister told us there were Home Children coming, I asked for a girl from Scotland, so I'm glad to get you. D'you come from a big family?'

Shyly, Jane told her about her parents losing little Peter and Owen then about her parents dying.

'I've still got two brothers and a sister but I haven't seen them for a long time.'

'Well, we all have to make the best of things. We'll help each other out. You've got a new life here: it's hard work on the farm, but it'll be good for you, and quite a change from old Glasgow. You'll need some working clothes, mind - keep your dress and pinafore for church.' The rest of the afternoon was spent finding something suitable for Jane to wear. Mrs O'Brien took an old cotton dress of her own and, with huge steel scissors, she cut it down to size. 'This'll get you started and we can get some more later. Go try it on.' Jane changed from her familiar clothes into the work dress. It was far too wide, so Mrs O'Brien fashioned a belt of sorts from the discarded material and tied it round her waist. She gave her an old straw hat, stitched to fit her head, and her outfit was complete. 'Let's have a look around now, so you can get your bearings.' Jake had been lying under the table, but as soon as the door was opened he got up and trotted beside Mrs O'Brien to join them on their walk. Jane was shown the toilet cubicle in the yard. Nearby was a round brick structure with a wooden contraption on top which turned out to be the well. 'We pump water up every day. You'll use it when you're doing the laundry.'

Then came the stable where the horse stood in its pen. Mrs O'Brien put some hay from a pile on the floor into a bucket and put it in beside him. Next was the barn, which felt hot, and smelled of something sweet and sickly that caught at the back of Jane's throat. Huge racks rose from floor to ceiling and were filled with what looked like long, dried grass. 'This is where we dry out the hay after harvest, to keep for animal feed. If we have to bring in extra workers, they sleep in here too. We had two Home boys who stayed for a few years till they were old enough to move on and my boys could take over the work of the farm.' While she was talking, they walked to an outbuilding which was full of stalls and had rows of buckets against the wall, and huge barrels. 'This is where the cows come to be milked and where they live in winter. You've missed the milking today but you can help me tomorrow.' Jane's heart sank. *How could she help with that?*

Last stop was a small shed with wire fencing round it, making what looked like a tiny garden. 'This here's the hen-house. Let's see if they've laid any eggs for us.' Mrs O'Brien stepped easily over the low fencing and Jane awkwardly followed her. When the woman opened the door, a terrible squawking started up and two large, fat, brown birds began flapping their wings. They flew out onto the ground and Jane cowered back. As they pecked the ground, they shook small red flaps on the top of their heads which made them look very angry, but thankfully they ignored Jane. Mrs O'Brien leaned into the shed and took a tin bowl from a bundle on a shelf. Then she rustled the hay along several racks and emerged with six eggs in the bowl. Jane was amazed. She had only ever seen eggs in the grocer's or in the cupboard at home. She'd never questioned where they'd come from. 'This'll be a job for you too, Jane. Here, carry this for me.' She handed Jane the bowl of eggs, and back at the house showed her the pantry where fresh food was stored.

At tea time, the boys came in from their work in the fields. Mrs O'Brien served up and said Grace, 'For what we're about to eat, may the Lord make us truly thankful.' Jane answered 'Amen' with the others. Over huge slices of fresh bread and cheese with pickles, Jane observed the family while they chatted about their day. Robbie looked like an older version of Jimmy. They both had blue eyes and fair hair, burned golden from the sun - their arms and faces were tanned a dark brown and their hands were rough. They seemed nice and were polite to their mother. Their accents sounded more like Miss Bilbrough and the people who worked at Marchmont. As they chattered on, Jane's eyes began to close and her head drooped. 'Time you were in bed, I think. You can get to the toilet from the door in your room and I've left a lamp lit for you to carry with you,' said Mrs O'Brien. Jane said goodnight.

When she was in her room with the door closed, she took the lamp from the table and opened the back door. The yard was now dark and the toilet seemed far away. Just then, from round the side of the house, Jake's paws sounded on the gravel and he came and nudged at her with his head till she patted him. He walked with her to the toilet and, when she came out, he followed her into her room. When she changed into her nightdress and got under the quilt, he flopped on the floor beside her bed - she put her hand out and patted his head again.

The warmth coming from him was comforting. 'Thanks, Jake', she whispered and fell fast asleep.

38

Jane was awakened by a loud, piercing, shrieking noise coming from the yard which was immediately followed by Jake barking in response: she sat up, bewildered. Mrs O'Brien came in, laughing. 'That's our cock crowing. You won't sleep in with him around. Get dressed and come through for breakfast.' Jane could smell porridge and toasted bread. It was appetising, and she washed and dressed then hurried to the table. She couldn't believe she was hungry after the food she'd eaten the day before.

'Morning.' chorused the boys.

'Morning.' They ate and Mrs O'Brien said,

'We'll be going to church this morning and you'll have Sunday School, so you can change into your Sunday clothes after you fetch in the eggs. Remember how I showed you yesterday?' Jane nodded nervously as Mrs O'Brien held out a small paper bag which rustled as she handed it over. 'Here - you can scatter this grain outside the shed, but inside the wire, for them to eat.' After breakfast, Jane went out to the yard. She stepped over the wire fence and scattered the grain, but had to summon up all her courage to open the door of the hen-house. She pulled it open and jumped to the side as the birds came rushing out. They completely ignored her again and she felt more relaxed about searching on the racks for eggs. After putting them in the bowl, they were delivered to the pantry. 'Well done,' said Mrs O'Brien, 'looks like you're a fast learner - we'll try you with the cows later.'

When they were all dressed smartly for church, they got into the wagon. With only just room for the four of them on the bench, Jane was squeezed in between Mrs O'Brien and Jimmy. Robbie took the reins this time, his strong muscles flexing as he drove the horse along. They stopped at the church on the edge of the township and Robbie tied the horse to a post. People nodded as they passed, some calling out good morning; others looked closely at Jane and muttered under their breath. Inside, at the back of the church, a group of children were gathered round a young woman in a cotton dress and a white straw hat from which dark curls were escaping. Mrs O'Brien approached her.

'This is Jane who's come to live with us from Scotland, Miss Allison. I'll collect her after the service.'

'Of course, Betty.' She took Jane's hand.

'I'm Miss Allison, your Sunday School teacher. We do our lessons downstairs. Come along, children.' The group followed her down a staircase. The room they went into had chairs arranged in a circle, with a hymnal on each seat. Jane was given the seat next to Miss Allison.

'Have you been to church before, Jane?'

'Yes, Miss, but not Sunday School. We got all our lessons at the Home.' She was aware of the other children looking at her intently.

'I see. Well, that sure is excellent. We're going to read some stories from the Bible and sing some hymns, so just join in when you can.' Jane was pleased to be able to sing some of the hymns and say the Lord's Prayer at the end. When they got upstairs, the adults were just coming out, so Miss Allison took her over to Mrs O'Brien.

'She did well, Betty. See you next week, Jane.'

'Well, that's a relief,' said Mrs O'Brien, Let's get home now.' They got back to the farm in time for dinner. Jane changed into her work dress and helped lay the table with dishes and cutlery from the dresser. Afterwards, she washed the dishes in a tub in the pantry and put them away. Mrs O'Brien looked pleased. 'We don't do laundry on a Sunday and it's too soon to milk the beasts, so you can rest for a while. It wouldn't do you any harm to read that nice bible you've got. We'll be in the sitting-room off the kitchen if you need us.' Jane read her bible for a while before going to the toilet across the yard; she smiled as Jake appeared at her side carrying an old ball. He sat at the door till she came out, then dropped the ball at her feet. *How funny he was.* Jimmy joined them in the yard and laughed at the antics of the dog. 'He wants you to throw his ball for him. Look.' He took the ball and threw it across the yard. Jake sprinted, with tail wagging, to retrieve it and lay it at Jimmy's feet. 'Over to you, Jane, but stop when you want. He'll have you playing all day otherwise.' She spent an exhilarating hour throwing the ball for Jake, who never seemed to tire of fetching it. Following her into the house, he lay down beside her bed and she sat down to read some more.

She felt happy that she'd made a friend, even if he wasn't human; she patted his head and he licked her hand, looking up at her.

Later in the afternoon, Mrs O'Brien called Jane out into the yard. Robbie and Jimmy were walking beside a dozen cows which were heading for the milking shed. Jane stood against the wall as they passed, aghast at how enormous the cows were and how dirty they looked close up. Once the cows were in the stalls of the shed, the brothers left and Mrs O'Brien led Jane inside. It was hot and smelly - Jane felt she might not be able to breathe for long. Mrs O'Brien went into the first stall and sat on a stool beside the cow, close up to its side. 'Fetch me a bucket and stand beside me.' Then, standing terrified beside the fearless woman, Jane watched in astonishment as Mrs O'Brien put her hands beneath the cow and began pulling at pink, dangling bits of flesh. They were attached to what looked like swollen, dirty white bags. Within seconds, milky fluid sprayed down into the bucket. Jane waited for the cow to retaliate by attacking her or Mrs O'Brien but it stood patiently letting the milking go on.

'Is that not sore for the cow?' Jane asked.

'Not a bit. It's a relief for it to get rid of the milk - it's heavy to carry about. Fetch me another bucket.' When Jane returned, she swapped her the empty bucket for the full one. 'Pour this into the first barrel in the row, Jane.' Mrs O'Brien began milking again, and when no more milk came from the cow she moved to the next stall. After milking them all, she called for Robbie and Jimmy to take them back to their field. 'One day soon, you'll be able to do this for me.' Jane really could not imagine this; however, as the weeks went by she picked up many skills.

On weekdays, she did the family laundry: carrying water from the well; heating it in the enamel bath; washing the clothes and hanging them out. As she was too small to reach the line, Robbie made her a box to stand on. Her life couldn't have been more different from the life she'd led in Glasgow, but she soon felt part of the rhythm of the farm. School was attended now and again, if someone had time to run her to the township.

After a few weeks, Mrs O'Brien said,

'We're pleased with you, Jane. We've decided we're going to keep you, so you'll be here till you grow up. How d'you feel about that?'

'Good, thank you, Mrs O'Brien. I'd like that.'

'And if you feel comfortable with it, you can call me Mother now.' Jane hesitated for a moment, thinking about Roseanne, her ma, whom she'd never called Mother; it didn't feel like she was betraying her, so she nodded. Jane could see that Mrs O'Brien had suffered loss like her and they could help each other; her heart warmed at the idea of her new life ahead.

Extracts from Inspection Records:

<u>December 1879. G.L. visited.</u>
Janie writes, 'I send you these few lines to let John know that I am well. I like this country better than the old one. I love Mother and the boys and Jake. I go to school and Sunday School. My love to Mrs Quarrier and the family. I should like my brother John to write to me. Tell my brother that I pray for him and I hope he will be a good man. I have sent him a tract that I like, '*Seek and ye shall find me.*'

<u>September 1881. By Rev. C. Watch.</u>
When I visited, I found Jane had just returned from school very happy. She said she would not like to return to the Home and leave Mrs O'Brien. In reading, she is on the second book.

<u>July 7th, 1882. By Mrs I.E.Q.</u>
Janie is the picture of health and happiness and is evidently much liked in her home. Mrs O'Brien had lost her husband and four children within a year and wanted a little one to fill up the blank. Janie does not remember anything at all about Scotland or the Home. Goes to Church, Sunday School and day school.

<u>May 3rd 1883. By R. Wallace.</u>
Jane is a nice-looking girl, very useful and much loved by Mrs O'Brien. She is the only girl in the family.

See Author's note, Page 181.

Author's note

Between 1869 and 1939, over 120,000 children, some as young as four, were sent to Canada, as part of various child migration schemes, from all over the United Kingdom. Their descendants make up over 10% of the current Canadian population. Thousands more went to other Commonwealth countries. Many churches and charitable organisations took part in what was often referred to as 'The Golden Bridge'. Though many settled well and had good lives, there were many reported cases of abuse of the children involved. Many of the children were not, in fact, orphans, but were considered to be at risk living with their natural parents. Once in Canada, many of them were not sent to school. Older children, who became indentured workers, often did not receive any wages. The younger ones, although often living as part of families, were not formally adopted, as Canadian adoption legislation was not passed until much later, in the 20th Century. Census returns on Jane recorded her as being a domestic servant till she was 21. In 1897, Ontario passed an 'Act to regulate the immigration into Ontario of certain classes of children'. It required each Home to have a licence and to keep up-to-date records of the movements, habits and well-being of every child in its care. William Quarrier did not agree with this, arguing that his methods had little in which to find fault. He felt that he was being punished for the failure of other organisations and withdrew from the scheme for one year, but later re-commenced his work of sending children abroad. In all, over 7,000 children went from Quarrier's Homes in Scotland to Canada. In recent years, several governments and organisations, including Quarriers, have apologised to child migrants, their families and their descendants for any physical or emotional abuse they may have suffered over the years.